SPIKE BROWN

SHERLOCK HOLMES
THE WHEELCHAIR MOB

ILLUSTRATED BY

KARL WHITELEY

Tower Bridge
Books

Tower Bridge Books

A catalogue record of this book is available from the British Library

For Gail & Sally

221B, Holmes ponders the serious case of the Wheelchair Mob, with Mrs. Hudson in attendance

"Marfa," he yelled to the lady pianist. "Strike up the band, it's the funeral march I'd quite fancy 'earin'. Nice an' slow, like. Go orn, play it loud, my gal." Alf twisted round, heading for the door. "Keep out of my way the pair o' you plain clothes. I got business to attend to."

The music started to play. The discordant, clumsy notes of that old faithful dirge proved strangely apt, for if he had only known, he had but a short time to live.

"Alf's got a shooter," someone screamed, "and if 'e gets riled 'e'll use it."

The pub door swung open, allowing in light and a freezing draught, and the powerfully built disabled man manoeuvred his wheeled chair with an awkward shove of his shoulders onto the first step, the rusty revolver still present on his lap. No sooner had he done so when from what we could gather, peering tentatively out of the window, police started to open fire from the top storey of the terraced house opposite. Alf died almost instantly in a hail of bullets, the distinctive tune of the funeral march accompanying the deadly racket that ensued. Eventually, his battered, lopsided wheelchair keeled over and toppled down the steps, drunkenly spilling the ruined body of the once popular character, known and well-liked in the community of Bethnal Green, out onto the wintry, icy precinct of Drake Street.

The eerie pall of confused and shocked silence that hung over the public bar was palpable. The acrid stench of cordite and gun smoke still permeated the air. A woman's voice, polite and without undue emotion, broke the prevailing mood.

"It's him, Inspector Lestrade. Alfred Hornsby, the man who conspired with the others to murder my husband." ...

1

How significant that, during what came to be one of the most fraught episodes in Mr Sherlock Holmes' career, a dense ochre fog smothered the capital, refusing to abate for a full fortnight. Even our globe lamps, lit early as befits early November, for some reason of low gas pressure, shone but weakly casting an insipid glow; a gloomy, depressing ambience about our front sitting room which befitted the presence at our lodgings of two unwanted visitors presently slouched on the sofa.

Possessing the appearance of a couple of Soho dandies: Jack Cawdaw, sporting a gold pocket watch, skull fob, death-head rings on every finger, wore a lilac bowler and spats and the most loud, vulgar, yellow-checked suit I ever saw. His accomplice, Archie Troughton, sporting equally garish attire: a gold, glittery waistcoat, shod in leopard-skin hobnail boots, reeking of Bay rum, his hair, I recall, centre parted, plastered flat.

Cawdaw was putting forward a truly odious proposal. "You owe us," said he, "the debt must be paid in full, five hundred quid for starters. You're a successful man of means, Mr Holmes. This request is in no way unreasonable considering what was achieved. The amount of jobs you and Wiggins employed us on for nothing but bleedin' coins. I risked my neck, remember, for tanners an' halfpennies."

"The problem," said I, stubbing out my cigar, like my esteemed colleague remaining calm and steady, outwardly amenable, for to become annoyed, form rash pronouncements was unwise in present company, "is that unlike Wiggins, now an officer cadet training at Sandhurst Academy or, say, Billy, Mrs Hudson's devoted page for a number of years after leaving his post employed first as a city messenger, assiduously attended night classes gaining personal tuition."

"Paid for by Mr Holmes."

"Certainly, and thereafter has become an assistant manager at a carpet shop in Tooting and is engaged to be married; the money Holmes forwarded towards their welfare and education paid dividends but, and I say this in all seriousness Jack, money, whatever the amount, was not in itself what advanced their careers and earning capacity – rather, hard work and application. In all honesty, pimping, drug dealing and worse crimes, which I believe you both embrace with considerable alacrity, lacks a way forward for negotiation. Only last month, Cawdaw, I read about your attendance at a police court."

"Point taken, but the fact remains Mr Holmes owes us, for the second time of asking, five hundred quid in notes. Where's the harm?"

I cannot for the life of me convey adequately the terrible stalemate that existed that afternoon in our rooms. Like tenacious pit-bull terriers, our visitors remained one-purposed, miscreants hardened, since the age of eight years, to a life of crime, well-versed to street life and debauchery, denizens of the gaudy gin palaces, variety hall, opium dens, the greyhound track and much, much worse, their vicious personalities formed upon neighbourhood violence and extortion remained stubbornly resilient, but Holmes persisted.

"I refuse your demands utterly. I am naturally rather un-keen to contribute to funding your womanising and nefarious low-life rackets. Jack, Archie, think again I beg you. If only you were legitimate, honest painters and decorators, brickies, clerks in the city, I should be able to advance a guinea or two. As it is ..." Both my colleague and I remained on our guard.

"Very well," said the rascal frowning. "But Ralph Brown won't like, nor appreciate, your attitude. He expected, like us, to be dealing with a wiser, a more sensible individual open to ..."

"Persuasion, corruption? I think not."

"Ralphy," said I, all of a sudden remembering a little bright urchin with a grubby face, a glimmer of joy in my heart. "Ralph Brown, a Baker Street Irregular, just like yourselves. Didn't he hurt himself? Got injured outside the market at Billingsgate – a carriage accident?"

"Mr Brown, one might say, was nonchalantly crippled for life. He's in a wheeled chair, has been these last three years or so. A toff, bloody nob ran 'im over crossing the street – left Ralph for dead."

"But what's his part in this visit of yours?" asked Holmes, puffing on his old, black clay. "What's he got to do with all this obtaining money, why has Brown to be consulted? Don't tell me he is a rogue as well."

"You just have no idea of the bad feeling you're creating, Mr Holmes. Mr Troughton and I have been perfectly reasonable in our demands. The next time won't be so friendly. I said it once, an' I'll say it again ... you owe us."

"Nothing doing. That is my last word on the matter. Good day," Holmes reiterated.

My colleague smoked his pipe, leaning back in his armchair.

Cawdaw got up to leave as did his friend. Placing his lilac bowler at a jaunty angle upon his crop of blonde hair, he spoke with understated malevolence. "You owe us," he repeated.

The following morning found me annoyingly summoned from a fitful slumber by a piercing scream. I perceived, tiredly, that the noise emanated from the downstairs hall where our landlady's apartments were situated. More screams followed.

Grabbing my dressing gown, having heard Holmes rush out of his room, it soon became apparent Mrs Hudson was suffering some fit of hysteria, not brought on, I must hasten to add, by one of Holmes' chemistry outrages, not recently doing anything remotely irritable to upset our Scotch landlady or threaten our tenancy.

When I joined Holmes in the hall downstairs, however, a scene was in progress, Mrs Hudson being comforted, sobbing on my colleague's shoulder in a state of distress. My friend tactfully drew my attention to the partly open front door. Poking my head outside into fog-bound Baker Street I was confronted by the decomposed carcass of a mangy cat tied by a noose to the brass door knocker. The dreary fog only enhanced the unusual nature of this macabre trophy.

"There's a note – stuffed in the cat's mouth – be good enough to retrieve it, dear boy. Now, now, Mrs Hudson, do not overly concern yourself; the work of local miscreants, nothing more. By the by, I quite fancy curried chicken this morning, if I may, and a pot of your usual exemplary ground Brazilian coffee. Ham and egg, Watson?"

"Please," I enjoined, extricating the roll of grubby paper from between the cat's fangs, like Holmes, anxious to restore domestic equanimity as quickly as possible. "A rack of toast also, Mrs Hudson," I called out cheerfully as our landlady retreated to her ground floor apartment, her own personal domain, to recover from the shock, closing the door firmly behind her.

Still in my pyjamas, I requisitioned a down and out, an old vagrant passing the step, and by means of a sixpence enticed that same worthy into disposing of the disgusting dead cat in the nearest public waste bin. I duly hastened upstairs to our rooms and, giving the fire a poke to liven the flames, anxiously awaited the results of Holmes' perusal of the note. He stood close to the mantelpiece, reading the aforementioned scrawl. It did not make for a particularly pleasant appraisal.

'We wouldn't want your dear old Mrs Hudson meeting wiv a nasty accident now would we, sir, while out shoppin', or visitin' a friend. Broken 'ip, crushed vertebrae, busted leg, so terribly bovversome an' pain inducin'. £500 to be paid werry promptly or weel's fix her proper.

Mr Anon.'

"Should we take this East End babble seriously, Holmes? I confess I'm inclined to chuck it in the fire and have done – get on with breakfast."

"We cannot simply ignore the message. This is the work of one time Irregulars, that shining example of juvenile initiative that has now, it appears, spawned a rash of egregious enthusiasts bent on pursuing a life of crime. I must telegraph Lestrade at once; and not a word to Mrs Hudson regarding this filthy extortion business. She must remain wholly ignorant of the present threat against her well-being. The dead cat is dealt with, anyhow."

————

At a quarter past eleven, responding to Holmes' telegraph, Inspector Lestrade arrived at our rooms accompanied by a timid little bearded man clad from head to foot in black, hobbling awkwardly, leaning upon a rubber-tipped cane. I judged by his bandaged head and the way he winced when welcomed to sit upon the sofa his ribs had been fractured, the fellow evidently involved in a recent fracas.

It turned out Mr Gooch was an enterprising tailor by profession who had built up his business in the East London district of Horditch over a number of years, his premises referred to in those days as a sweat shop, being the employer of female labour stitching garments, crowded into a single room. However, the interview that followed proved remarkably enlightening, Lestrade offering an introduction.

"Mr Holmes, a wheelchair gang is gaining something of a notorious reputation in Horditch. Locals are much too scared to talk. Police so far have garnered little useful intelligence. The gang remain an enigma, yet residents must face the unwanted rise of a new kind of thug emerging on the streets. Mr Gooch, pray enlighten these gentlemen as to how you came about those injuries. Mr Holmes is a consulting detective and may be able to assist."

"Well, I was approaching the pedestrian tunnel what the railway runs over when, I svear, aht the fog they come, monstrous thugs – beefy, broad-shouldered rascals wearing Injun fevvers an' rough-stitched leather masks. Gawd, I gets nightmares jest finkin' abaht 'em. In wheeled chairs they was. Sawn orf shotguns strapped to the armrests; hemmed me in against a brick wall, snatched me takings, punched me in the gut, laid me flat aht in the gutter leaving me fer dead. I reckon if it weren't for a passin' pleesman I wouldn't be 'ere nah. I've neffer seen anyfink like it, guvnor. Mobsters in wheeled chairs spinnin' on the axis like the chairs wuz a part of 'em. I ask yer – armed to the bloody teef wiv guns. Wass the worl' comin' to?"

"Now, Inspector, I beg you consider this newspaper article scissored from an old copy of the Daily Telegraph. I file away such leaders with good purpose."

Lestrade duly considered the proffered article, puffing on his cigar all the while. I offer an accurate facsimile below for the discerning reader.

'We regret to report in this newspaper the sad news of the sudden death of Lord Smith, the wealthy society figure known and loved by this correspondent who readers of this column will recall I reported was involved in a minor road accident when the victim, an unemployed poor of no consequence, a Ralph Brown, was crushed beneath His Lordship's fine landau not far from Billingsgate market. His Lordship, thank goodness, escaped injury and none of his grooms or fine chestnut mares suffered from the incident. However, it pains me to report Lord Smith was discovered yesterday dismembered in an alley off Berwick Street in Soho. Police continue to make inquiries. His Lordship was apparently last seen entertaining a jolly club, the Wages of Sin, accompanied by a male colleague, in fine fettle. He mentioned to this correspondent with his usual grace and impeccable composure that he was going on to the Reform later for supper.'

"I recall the case," remarked Lestrade. "The Wages of Sin in Berwick Street has a seedy, immoral reputation and the murder was put down to possibly an altercation concerning blackmail, a toff's severe roughing-up which got out of hand. Bradstreet was the officiating officer."

"Dismemberment – that should require a group of ruffians, surely. What if anything similar should be planned for dear Mrs Hudson? Holmes, we must act ..."

"I cannot but agree, Watson, upon this occasion you are correct. We require a second-hand wheeled chair, additionally filthy, evil-smelling apparel from a rag shop, an amount of theatrical grease applied to our faces, false wigs, Piccadilly whiskers and – bravo – a change of identity. You are Fred Gnoball, my long-suffering friend and helper; I am to be Jobe Carter, ex-railway worker now a crook confined to a wheeled chair due to a shunting accident. Watson, if you will be good enough to occasionally push the contraption once we take the train to Horditch. Any decent pubs in that vicinity, Mr Gooch?"

"Why, sir, ve Earl of Berkeley stands on a corner, ve White Hart upon anuvver an' a gin palace along ve 'Igh Street."

"Excellent. We shall, by this afternoon, have established ourselves in the East End parish of Horditch, and our work begin in earnest," said Holmes.

The Scotland Yarder got up to leave, Mr Gooch painfully getting back on his feet.

"I admire your nerve, Mr Holmes," remarked Lestrade. "Horditch – forgive me, Mr Gooch, no disrespect, is an abysmal place of overcrowded slums, doss houses and sweat shops. There is a gasworks and an India rubber manufactory. Hardly the most salubrious of districts."

————

Having purloined a cab in Baker Street, we travelled, with a large carpet bag for luggage, upon the London and Blackwall railway from Fenchurch Street, with all the noise and smoke of the engine darting over the bridge crossing the Minories, thence along a smoky viaduct set amid slate roofs and chimneys of the grimy, soot- encrusted, closely-knit terraced houses of East London. The train stopped at Bethnal Green Road before continuing onward past the recreational park to Old Street until we attained Horditch, thereafter disembarking, bracing ourselves to face the damp, chill fog of a November afternoon.

Not far from the station was a rag shop possessing a yard heaped with old sticks of furniture and other assorted risible junk. Thus the proprietor, disinterested, more concerned with sorting items of old chinaware, provided us with ideal disguises. Additionally, a suitable third- or fourth-hand invalid chair with a high-backed, basket weave seat was forthcoming for the price of a mere five shillings. Not long afterwards, we discovered why it was sold us so cheaply, for the rim of one of the wheels was buckled, necessitating me, when pushing, to grip the handles very tightly. Even so, its tendency to scrape into walls, to nearly pitch Holmes onto the pavement, was a bind of the first order.

Earlier, concealed in a rubbish-strewn alley, Holmes had managed to apply his considerable theatrical make-up skills to transforming us from middle- to lower-class citizens. We emerged not as top hatted, booted and suited city gentlemen, but rather with the appearance of the most ragged, ill- dressed, filthy pair of scoundrels this side of the river.

Our first choice of hostelry was to be The Earl of Berkeley, a clean, well-appointed public house on the corner of Martlet Street; evidently popular with locals, the place was packed and bustling with activity. "Vunder if I might 'ave a word," my colleague asked over a cacophony of raised voices, the clink of glasses, a pianola banging out a popular tune, having spied an opportune fellow sat amongst the crowd of punters supping his ale, though more pertinently using a wheeled chair. An approachable drinker, he warmed to my colleague at once.

"Course yer can, mate, Sid Bardon. Pint for boaf of yer?"

"Ta, India pale ale fer me, Wervingtons for 'im. Jobe Carter's the name. 'Ere, I wuz wonderin' wevver, Sid, you'se could put me right regardin' employment prospects. 'Ere's a quid fer yer trouble, like."

The other leant over, snatching the note and pocketing it. He grinned. "Well, Jobe, me ol' China, what yer 'arter?" said he, eyeing my colleague more cautiously, opening his pea jacket to reveal a wallet of pick-locks, a large Bowie knife and revolver wedged into a thick, studded belt encircling his waist.

"Safe crackin'," said my colleague; no further prompting proved necessary. We were amongst sympathetic souls, it seemed.

"'Onourable occupation to be commended, Jobe, a good, worthwhile trade to 'ave. Nah, seez ver door where I'm pointin'? Vat's where Mr Brown keeps 'is recruitment agency. Mr Brown is effer so wised up regarding work round 'ere. You local?"

"'Orditch born and bred. Me farver worked in ver gasworks."

"Well, Mr Brown will see you'se alright, old son. Barman'll show ya boaf the vay, understood? I'll call 'im over."

The crowded public bar was full of a smog of choking tobacco fumes, the walls and ceiling dripping with condensation. Above the chatter, a self-playing pianola banged out a popular tune, 'Roll out the Barrel'. The barman showed us discreetly into a back room where only one person was present. Facing us was a giant of a fellow, massively built, with a thick neck.

Our interviewer was possessed of broad, muscular shoulders. Sat in a wheeled chair, he wore an immaculately tailored frock coat, although the upper half of his face was concealed by an unusual tribal mask; stitched rough leather woven with Red Indian feathers whose effect was, frankly, unnerving. The chap placed a sheaf of papers in front of him, licking the end of a lead pencil.

"Name?"

"Jobe Carter."

"And 'im – yer mate?"

"Fred."

"Name's Brown. You heffer done any bloke a violence?"

"Course I 'ave," Holmes answered, a sneer of contempt for the question darkening his grubby, bovine features. "Plenty of 'em. Broke boaf of Skiff's legs wiv a bit o' lead pipin' an' crushed 'ees skull to a pulp fer good measure. Remember vat one, Fred?"

"Cor blimey," said I, mustering my very best cockney accent, mimicking Holmes somewhat. "'Ow could I heffer forget? Weren't vat Jimmy Skiff from ver East India vot called yer 'a useless cripple' to yer face?"

"Bloody right. I done 'im, venn Fred weighted 'im dahn wiv a granite bird barf – chucked 'im in ver canal. No bovver."

"Jobe, ole son, I'm gettin' to like you more an' more. I fink we might 'ave a vacancy. Show us yer lead." From his long understanding of underworld slang, Holmes coughed and drew back his blanket, causing our interviewer's mouth to gape open in astonishment.

"Bloomin' 'eck – machine pistol an' a sawn off Purdey tied to eiffer armrest. 'Ow do vey fire?"

"Nice an' accurate, bootifully crafted them Purdeys h'aint vey," Holmes laughed raucously. "See, I even got a cord what I pulls down 'ere somewhere if I wants to fire 'em boaf togevver."

"Where you get that la di dah Purdey, any'ow? Corst a flippin' arm an' a leg don't vey. Torfs' guns I calls 'em."

"Nicked in an 'ouse job down Bermondsey way."

"Alright, I've written down yer details. Got any decent references I can call in?"

"Jeb Baines doin' a stretch at Pentonville'll vouch fer me. Sharky Trentor incarcerated fer five years on Dartmoor will verify my talents as a first-class

cracksman. Pete 'The Cosh' is presently doin' time at
..."

"Alright, that'll do. 'Ere, tell you what – we got a big job comin' up. I'll see if we got a vacancy, 'ow's vat? Come and see me at the end of the week."

"When's this job? I'm a bit short of farvings, Mr Brahn."

"P'raps next mumph – don't you worry, Jobe, I'll see you an' Fred alright, you're jest the sort I'm arter. That gunnery of yours'll come in werry 'andy."

Once outside, surveillance was now imperative. Ridding ourselves of that old five bob rickety wheeled chair by means of hurling the risible contraption over a wall onto some waste ground, after, that is, retrieving our carpet bag, placing the valuable guns from Holmes' Museum collection inside to join our neatly folded gentlemen's attire and box of theatrical make-up, we remained poised over the road, hidden behind a hedge. The East End fog hampered visibility somewhat. Mr Brown must be investigated further, and to this end we took up positions on the opposite side of the street concealed behind shrubbery. The illumination of a nearby row of wrought- iron lamps, the windows of The Earl of Berkeley over the road lit by gas jets, meant we were able to observe the various comings and goings. At a quarter to ten, Mr Brown slipped out by a side door. A grown adult, no longer the chirpy street urchin I remembered, I confess I found little in his persona to link him to young Ralph, the mask of course prohibitive, the voice entirely changed. Sat in his wheeled chair, his feathered leather mask incredibly still in place, this tribal emblem a powerful reminder of his criminal allegiance to be no doubt respected and feared by the folk of Horditch, for surely the innovative gang's headquarters was that same back room at The Earl of Berkeley pub. The fog both aided and hampered our advance. "We must remain vigilant, follow Mr Brown,

Watson," proposed my companion hugging close to the wall, keeping alert to the sound of creaking basketwork, a squeaky wheel as the contraption trundled along the pavement from one wrought- iron gas lamp to the next, the powerful upper torso of the sitter providing rapid locomotion.

"So, he heads down Fenn Street, along Gasworks Road." Our shabby appearance meant any passing pedestrian paid no heed. We blended in entirely with the social strata evident in this down-at-heel neighbourhood, that poor and destitute district of East London.

"I can just about make out the gasworks," said I, peering through the fog at the shadowy gasometers looming further up on the right. A chimney stack marked the India rubber factory, the lingering effluvium smothering the streets and back-to-back tenements of Horditch, an ever present reminder of industry at its very worst.

"Now, Watson, we perceive Brown has disappeared inside that mission building. Ah, now he ventures forth from the front entrance, an oil lamp clipped to his machine. He now heads west towards the gasworks."

"We follow."

"I think not – I think it preferable to pause a while …"

Having advanced further along the pavement it was now patently obvious that the old mission had been converted into offices for a local solicitor. The brass plaque stated his name was Edward Lambart, Commissioner of Oaths, and this was where Brown had visited briefly.

"You intend to break in," said I, understanding his radical approach.

"Just so, my dear fellow, I shall be back presently. Stay put while I utilise my trusty pipe knife levering the latch of a sash window. You will, I trust, keep a sharp lookout for beat constables. The last thing we require is arguing with a desk sergeant and spending a wasted night in a police cell arrested for attempted burglary."

"Very well, Holmes," I answered, assailed by the stringent odour emanating from the rubber works that clung to hair and clothing. My eyes and throat were certainly irritated. Evidently, the manufactory was a twenty-four-hour concern, the furnaces manned round the clock.

Presently, Holmes emerged at the front entrance and, once inside the office, we began an immediate, but painstaking search of the neat and tidy room inhabited by the solicitor. Most drawers and cupboards were securely locked, but my colleague, in a masterly act of observing minutiae, drew my attention to something I should have myself ignored and not bothered with.

"A wall calendar."

"What of it?" said I, dismissively, my gaze set upon finding a certain damning document as I rummaged atop of the desk, the meagre glow from a street lamp outside allowing us enough light to see by.

"Informs us of much."

"Really, Holmes, do get a move on – informs us of what?"

"Watson, don't procrastinate so, come over here and let me hear what you make of this. I apologise for such trifling inconsequential clues; the dates, you will perceive, clearly ringed in green ink – are?"

"Second of December, twelfth of December, eighteenth of that month," I remarked irritably.

"The writing indicates?"

"One reads 'Uncle Samuel visits', another 'Aunt Heywood for luncheon', the last 'young Middleton supper engagement at club'."

"Which is superlatively crucial to our investigation. You know my methods by now. For heav- en's sake, man, let us hear your views – expand."

I mustered my thoughts and proposed what I believed to be perfectly sound. "Mr Edward Lambart's relatives, else acquaintances, are members of this gang you could infer. They regularly meet here at the ex- mission, at certain times every month – planners, organisers – possibly the brains of the enterprise, the solicitor and not Ralph Brown at the helm of the criminal body as we at first supposed."

Even through his heavily applied bovine make- up I could see my companion appeared somewhat scathing. "My dear fellow, far be it for me to criticise your somewhat marginal conclusions, not without merit, incidentally, though mostly erroneous," Holmes elaborated. "Suffice to say, the written names on the calendar refer to chains of jewellers popular in London and the provinces. H. Samuel & Co., Heywoods, Middletons – surely you must have seen the shops endemic in every district, Old Street being the closest. I perceive by the expression of utter amazement on your grubby, bewhiskered features, you have caught on at long last."

"Indeed I have, old chap. This indicates the wheeled chair mob are about to launch a series of extraordinary gem heists."

"Elementary, but how exactly? I mean, surely their mobility is limited."

"Well, Holmes, we are due to revisit The Earl of Berkeley at the end of the week."

"Without the slightest regret. I fear, my dear Watson, our wheeled chair days are well and truly over.

Most assuredly we have seen the last of Jobe Carter and his trusty confidante, Fred. To venture back to Mr Brown's secure territory ignoring the possibility he may have indeed checked my references and found them entirely contrived and bogus is most unwise. I should prefer to work out how exactly this gang propose to rob the first jewellers, the raid planned for the second of December – a branch of H. Samuel & Co., as indicated by the office calendar."

The following morning, we were weary of the interminable fog blanketing the metropolis, the view from our bay window presenting a profusion of shiftless, yellow contagion so dense it muffled the clatter of horse buses, hansom cabs and further carriage traffic passing beneath.

I, by diversion, continued to peruse my new edition of The Lancet comfortably ensconced before the cheery fire burning in the grate. A full half hour elapsed before next I considered the figure of my esteemed fellow lodger, wearing his purple dressing gown, hunched forward in his armchair studying a large-scale map, choosing his long cherry wood pipe from the rack, a stash of the black shag he preferred being readily close to hand. The jewellery shop raid problem continued to absorb his keen interest for most of the morning, a pile of reference works, guide books and large- scale maps piled up, else spread out over the carpet.

"Well, my dear Watson," he said at length, "you rightly intimate the solicitor Edward Lambart is involved. Was it he who recruited a number of disabled? Is it his diabolical vision of extorting money out of me that we presently languish under? From my file of legal indices that help me keep pace with the backgrounds of solicitors and barristers currently in practice, he is apparently highly successful in police custody cases, pouncing upon legal loopholes, bamboozling detectives with his clever jargon, being more than able to get his clients 'off the hook', to use the slang term, upon a fairly regular basis."

"Siding with, and sympathetic to, the criminal classes," said I.

"Naturally, and now owns the dubious privilege of becoming a king amongst knaves, recruiting various thuggish talents such as, presumably, Ralph Brown, who should have learnt much under my tutelage as a Baker Street Irregular, more's the pity, for he is evidently a lieutenant to be looked up to by the likes of

Cawdaw and Troughton. But I am entirely confused; the limitation of mobility confounds me still," said he, steepling his fingers together, stretching his long, lanky legs across the hearth rug. "How curious is it that the rubber works may yet yield a vital lead."

"What, that place?" said I, astounded. "A foul, smoke-belching edifice – I don't follow." I was still bristling at the remembrance. "It's a blight on the health of those living in the vicinity of Horditch. My eyes and throat still sting after our brief foray into the district. Kamens is apparently the largest producer of garden hosepipes in London, but to what cost? As a medical man, I cannot but condone such a manufactory. The moulding process, continuous production round the clock – but, forgive me, Holmes, what has the rubber works got to do with all this?"

"A major local employer certainly, where a man may earn his bread. A large factory, furnace house, most portentous. My dear Watson, I now know exactly the plan the wheeled chair mob intend to pursue when robbing the first jewellery shop on the list at Old Street. I must wire Inspector Lestrade without delay. Dear me, it appears a visit to Bradleys the tobacconist is in order,

for my supply is diminished and I am clean smoked out
of black shag."

2

The parish of Old Street is dominated by the venerable ancient tower of a former fifteenth-century church, a newer place of worship, and the town hall, the High Street, or Tarn Street typical of many serving the East End community consisting of a compact row of shops, the bespoke jeweller situated between a post office and a greengrocer in easy distance of the station, thus the railway's up and down lines forwarding to Horditch, the other direction onwards to Fenchurch Street.

"Lestrade," remarked Holmes whilst we were set to endure a further spell of a marathon four hour surveillance, for it was now approaching two in morning, and tempers were frayed, nothing remotely untoward having occurred. "I must insist you suspend critical judgement for the time being. We are, I am certain, gazing upon the very crux of the matter – the clever means as to how the robbery is to be achieved."

"I've seen absolutely nothing interesting or remotely suspicious so far, Mr Holmes. Why I bothered to turn up and assign a contingent of officers to this ridiculous business of yours is a mystery. Really, Holmes, I hope this turns out worthwhile; my superiors will be most scathing if I end up wasting police time and resources, all for one of your notorious crackpot theories.”

Quite suddenly, Lestrade sprang to alertness, ceasing his habitual caustic asides, instead peering inquisitively at my colleague, straining his ears to catch a sound becoming ever more perceptible. All of us were aware of a steady beat of a locomotive, a chuff-chuffing, whereupon a tiny engine hauling a coal wagon, the top covered with secured tarpaulin, had emerged further up emitting a protracted sigh of steam and smoke; it halted a little distance from the deserted station. The fireman and driver clambered down, running back to the coal truck unfastening guy ropes, pulling at the canvas sheet.

“Inspector,” said Holmes excitedly, pointing ahead with his silver-topped cane, “need I remind you Old Street is but a secondary East London station, serving mostly persons bound for the city by day, one or two freight passing through at night – no signal box nor junction – a station, then, of marginal importance.

Porters at this hour being notably absent, the station master unlocks and begins his duties at five, in reasonable time to receive the first of the day's frugal scattering of passengers. However, I perceive we have presently an interloper, not part of the original London & Blackwall Railway."

I concur our party was about to witness a uniquely coordinated movement of men. A metal-hinged flap opened at the side of the railway wagon, normally incorporated for expelling loads of coal, although, somewhat surprisingly at this juncture, a steel ramp was released. Next, able bodied accomplices climbed over the side of the truck aiding their nefarious, hideously masked compatriots, allowing first one and, thereafter, a further five wheeled chairs, bristling with weaponry, to emerge so that, once manoeuvred beyond a gap in the fence across the road and onto the pavement, free movement was easily attained. They had planned meticulously. I recall a nondescript turning I had barely registered in all those hours of surveillance which, I was later to discover, led directly to a courtyard and alley to the rear of a number of high street shops – the jewellers included.

Not long after was a muffled explosion, later a convoy of wheeled chairs, each, this time, supplemented with a large, bulging corn-sack attached to the back, for H. Samuels must have surely been well and truly fleeced clean of every valuable in stock, the shop's front windows decimated, representing a huge haul and much profit for the thieves. They followed the exact same route back across the road to the stationary train. The sacks were loaded on first, thence wheeled chairs and their masked occupants, two at a time, were, by means of parking on the ramp, raised to a horizontal level by a rope and pulley system. We judged the whole heist had been satisfactorily completed in under twenty minutes, the tiny tank engine, this time shunting backwards along with its innocuous coal wagon, were off the scene very quickly.

"Your officers of the Crown are, I trust, armed? For, Inspector Lestrade, it would be sheer folly if they were not. My wire was emphatic on the point; to underestimate these gang members will cost dearly."

"We, the Metropolitans, are armed, as you say, my men stout-hearted fellows all, neither incompetent nor lacking leadership, our policy to surround and contain the gang, along with their ill-gotten hoard, offering by means of a loud- hailer an honourable surrender. None of these villainous rascals responsible for robbing the Old Street jewellers with that ingenious train idea will be allowed to escape summary justice. A lengthy stretch breaking rocks and oakum picking at Her Majesty's pleasure will be their deserved lot. After all, Mr Holmes, thanks to your marginal contribution they are about to be promptly caught red-handed in the coal wagon along with the stash of sparklers and plate upon their return to Horditch rubber works."

"Where in heaven's name did the thieves purloin that damn locomotive?" said I, still totally mystified. "'An interloper' you referred to earlier – what were you driving at exactly? Be more specific."

"My dear Watson," answered my friend, somewhat exasperated by my inability to grasp facts, "you will recall, old fellow, I consulted that large-scale map back at our digs. Lo and behold, I discovered the rubber factory, that is the immense yard possessed of a number of railway lines, and rows of coal bunkers besides. From this we can surmise, with some confidence, that W. H. Kamens and Co. possessed its very own works locomotive, also a supply of coal wagons – the gauge suitable for main-line running.

Hence, its nifty trip up the line past Bermondsey Road to Old Street – and our presence in the parish this early dawning."

"I must say, Mr Holmes," concluded Inspector Lestrade, passing round cigarettes, "I am much relieved your eccentric bequests were adhered to on this occasion. I cannot but applaud your sound reasoning."

3

A week or so later, the fog having lifted somewhat, bright bars of sunlight striking the mantelpiece, breakfast barely finished, Mrs Hudson showed into our rooms a personage well known to us. A Mr Ketton, one of the clerks in charge of lost property at London Bridge station, who, upon occasions if any article was found and handed in by an honest passenger, sought out my esteemed colleague for his expertise in tracing its owner.

Our visitor was introduced to the sofa by Holmes, whilst I poured a cup of coffee from the silver-plated pot.

"And pray, to what do we owe this foray into Marylebone, Mr Ketton? Your duties should normally, upon a Monday morning, discourage such outings unless you have a problem needs attending to much more intriguing than a mere lost umbrella, else mislaid billycock hat."

"I does, sir," said he, removing from his jacket pocket a scuffed calfskin jewel case of battered appearance. "This item was found by a lady upon the 8:43 service, calls at Brockley, Honour Oak Park an' New Cross Gate."

"My, it's a rare thing," said my colleague examining the case minutely, unclipping the hinged lid to reveal a maroon velvet lining, evident the clear indentation of a brooch. "Aspreys, no less. The faded gold leaf lettering and crest reveal the date to be 1798, so we can judge whatever piece of fine jewellery it contained must be very valuable indeed."

"Just what we at the office decided, a rare jewel, and more pertinently, it ain't where it should be for the case is empty. Course, that don't necessarily mean much in our line of work, Mr Holmes, the case may have long ago passed its usefulness, being old and tatty; the owner replaced it with an altogether new one, left it on the train, but even so, a niggling doubt remains, hence my superior, Mr Buttevant, the person in charge at London Bridge station's extensive lost property department, allowed me this morning to enquire further into the possibility of theft and criminal involvement."

"My dear Ketton," my friend insisted, snatching his pipe from the mantelpiece, "I think your department head wise. Allow me to keep the jewel case for the time being. Of course, should I uncover anything untoward I shall not hesitate to inform my contacts at Scotland Yard, your lost property department notified. The size of that indentation that snugly fitted the brooch indicates a gem of considerable worth. Aspreys, of course, may possess a record in their vaults."

Mr Ketton got up to leave, having drunk his coffee. "I am much indebted for your time, Mr Holmes. You have ably assisted us in the past, the American Colt handgun being most effectively dealt with, I recall. Good day, gentlemen. I shall see myself out."

"Well, old chap," said I, slumping into my fireside chair lighting a Bradleys. "Something, anyhow, to take your mind off that solicitor, Edward Lambart, whom you've been brooding over lately, he still not having been apprehended."

"Quite so, Watson. I shall require Mrs Hudson to place adverts in a multitude of daily newspapers. A tried and tested means of attracting a person who may have mislaid, else been relieved by criminal means of valuable property. It's worked before in the past and may yet prove fruitful, results forthcoming."

A couple of days later, an attractive middle- aged lady graced our front sitting room. Her name was Moira Normanton and she was married and resident in Brockley. She possessed two daughters, Lumina Jane and Zita Marie and the family had recently taken up residence in her late uncle's substantial detached villa, having been beneficiaries of his generous will.

"The jewel case I instantly recognised, from The Times advertisement offering readers a succinct description, as mine, Mr Holmes. Aspreys, the correct date, the oval shape and somewhat worn condition due to its great age, tally, but also now you inform me the inlaid silver brooch, the ruby heirloom itself, is absent. That is truly heartbreaking, but such mischief is to be expected."

"Oh, why do you say that?" said I, much intrigued.

"Gentlemen, bear with me, I know this will sound absurd, but I put it to you – can a ghost steal from a safe? Is a ghost capable of such actions? If so, the ghost of my late uncle, for whatever reason, is responsible for stealing the heirloom, for my husband and my children are convinced this was how the deed was done. They have themselves witnessed the ghost on a number of occasions. How the empty jewel case ended up on a train to London Bridge completely eludes me. Might I have a cigarette?"

"A ghost with the ability to open a safe is patently absurd," said Holmes offering Mrs Normanton a Bradleys from his silver case, "yet your hypothesis, madam, I find irresistible. How long has your valuable been missing?"

"Barely a week. Two dear lady friends of mine suggested we might address the problem by holding a séance to contact my late uncle, Mr Dunbridge Spettisberg, an antiquarian when alive, although I personally knew nothing of him until informed by a solicitor of our great, good fortune."

"Then, Mrs Normanton, without delay, I and my colleague, Dr Watson, must venture forth with you to Brockley and set your mind at ease. The brooch shall be difficult to recover, but by no means impossible. Time is of the essence. We must take a cab forthwith to London Bridge."

"My dear sir, I hardly need remind you 'phantasms' linger best during the hours of darkness. Should you not prefer a later visit?"

"Day or night is inconsequential to this complex affair. You have been successfully robbed of a valuable ruby, Mrs Normanton, and it is up to me to discover the perpetrator. I am a consulting detective after all. Before we leave, madam, one further point; if you, and presumably your family, had no idea of this existing uncle from south London, thus unaware of how he looked in life, how, pray, was your husband able to so surely identify his likeness to this unrestful shade?"

"Why, Mr Holmes, I'd better explain. The house we inherited in Brockley still contains much of my late uncle's furnishings and belongings collected over a lifetime. There is a portrait in oils, both gilt framed and glassed, that hangs above the fireplace in the sitting room. I grant you, by the look of him, a friendly and genial, bewhiskered old gentleman, the most unlikely of agitated spectres else vengeful haunters."

Our journey by passenger service from London Bridge to Brockley proved both pleasing and revealing, for Mrs Normanton insisted upon listing certain of the queer artefacts amassed, filling every room of the villa when she and her husband first took possession due to her late Uncle Dunbridge's mania for collecting. For instance, the skull purportedly belonging to Robespierre guillotined in Paris during the revolution, the fracture upon the jawbone where he had been struck by a bullet when arrested clearly evident, the supposed corn cob pipe of President Lincoln, also his tobacco jar, an autographed original manuscript of The Pit and the Pendulum by Edgar Allen Poe and much more besides.

"We shall have to sling most of it out," the lady proclaimed as our train steamed out of Honour Oak Park. "I and my daughters have a large bonfire planned in the back garden to burn a good deal of papers and so forth."

"Might it not be prudent to have the artefacts valued by Bonham's or Sotherby's?" I enquired, seriously. "You never know, Mrs Normanton, you might be surprised and make a few bob."

"Nonsense, Dr Watson," our fellow passenger laughed gaily. "Dunbridge Spittisberg, from what we now know of him from staff and neighbours, and my husband, Wooten, concedes this was a true gentleman eccentric, a committed antiquarian collector, if you will, endowed with more money than sense, guilty of filling the whole house from
top to bottom with worthless memorabilia and old curiosities, and I love him the more for that, although I do wish he wouldn't pester us so as a ghost."

"If I have anything to do with it," remarked Holmes, knocking out his pipe on his heel as the train drew in to Brockley, "your uncle's antiquarian ghost shall be laid to rest fair and square, sooner rather than later, Mrs Normanton."

A five minute walk brought us to an avenue where, along with other properties, stood a large and handsome white villa. We were shown in by a welcoming maid who received our hats and canes and fussed over Mrs Normanton.

"This is Mr Sherlock Holmes and Dr Watson, Mary. Please bring in the tea, could you?"

A page, a boy of fourteen or so, made himself useful by taking some letters to the post box as directed by the lady of the house. Upon entering the sitting room, beside the sofa, was a large doll's house, a hinged dog on wheels with further toys clustered nearby.

"My husband has a job in the city, Mr Holmes. He is an accountant and prospers well. We owned a house in Norbury before moving here, being so close to the capital suits us wonderfully."

"The play house for your daughters is spacious and well crafted," mentioned Holmes, kneeling down, peering in an amused way through the paneless windows, admiring the little wooden Swiss-style stools and table.

"A Mr Thornton, a woodworker, built the house to may husband's basic design. Lumina and Zita enjoy larking about inside."

"The ghost you mention appears where exactly?"

"Upon the staircase; it caused my husband to rush upstairs to our bedroom where I was brushing my hair before the mirror on my dressing table and lock the door. Poor Wooten was most disconcerted and refused to budge for ten minutes or so."

"Whence the study, where the safe is presumably kept, that room through here, was left unoccupied and the thief struck."

"The ghost, Mr Holmes, a phantasm of my late uncle. Wooten swears he glimpsed this ghost for himself, remember. And I assure you, sir, my husband is no fool, of a delicate turn of mind, susceptible or weak-willed. He saw what he saw and I believe him."

"I shall not argue the point. My dear Mrs Normanton, might I be allowed to look upstairs in the attic? You have lately no doubt adopted that place as a lumber room, perhaps a refuge for your uncle's unwanted clutter?"

"Why yes. I have, myself, had a rummage, but there is only junk to be found. Of course, Mr Holmes, over a number of months we have removed a vast amount of my uncle's possessions filling the rooms of the house up there."

"Just so, I shall be no more than five minutes; bear with me. Watson, before we attain the higher regions, be a good fellow and list in your pocket book the contents – both fixtures and fittings – of the doll's house. Mrs Normanton, when this is done, please will you and your maid lead the way.

After I had compiled a short list at my colleague's request, we ascended a number of flights of stairs to the top of the house, passing the servants' landing until we at last attained the attic. The maid, accompanied by Mrs Normanton, showed us into the storage area. The bare eaves, the roof above us, boasted cobwebs in profusion. The entire attic piled with cardboard boxes. Much old pottery shards and various bric-a-brac consistent to the eccentric collector, moved up here, no doubt, by Mrs Normanton to clear the downstairs rooms of her late uncle's clutter. What, I presumed, was the infamous skull of Robespierre, himself a victim of Madame Guillotine, perched on a shelf, grinning at us.

My colleague put all his energies into conducting a search, tearing open certain boxes, lifting dust sheets – inquisitively darting back and forth regardless of raising much dust. I perceived, after ten minutes, a distinctive crack of glass when his foot accidentally knocked against a teak container. Pausing, he nudged the toe of his Chelsea boot against it once more. A rattle emerged and an expression of pure satisfaction enveloped his wan, hawk-like features.

"I have it, Watson!" he exclaimed. "The method was dratted clever, but not so clever as I. Mrs Normanton, let us retire downstairs to the sitting room for afternoon tea and I shall explain to you exactly how the thief managed to burgle your husband's safe."

Once we settled, helping ourselves to thinly-cut cucumber sandwiches and a portion of seed cake, Mary, the maid, pouring from a pot of India blend, my companion relaxed upon the sofa, proving from his discourse both direct and to the point.

"We must apply the lantern slide principle," said he. "Earlier, upstairs in the attic, my foot most providentially struck the edge of a teak receptacle filled with tightly packed glass photographic plates. One of the emulsion developed plates cracked on impact. Consequently, randomly shifting a dust sheet, revealed, plain as day, a box camera with brass lens. Also tripod attachments, bottles labelled 'Emulsifier', various chemicals. Additionally, a stash of loose, boxed correspondence headed The Photographic Society of London, indicating assuredly your long-lost Uncle Dunbridge Spettisberg was an amateur photographer in life, possessing his very own dark room with the wherewithal to develop pictures at leisure. Furthermore, the society allowed him to indulge his hobby, being, on occasion, photographed for posterity by friends likewise minded to this new science. You follow me, Mrs Normanton?"

"Perfectly. You are accurate and concise, Mr Holmes. My late uncle did indeed possess a dark room in the basement of the house, which we cleared out. Dr Watson, more tea? Please continue your exciting recitation."

"Your accommodating daughters' play house, created of plywood, provides our next revealing clue as to how our thief struck. Positioned as the toy is, please note, when the sitting room door is wide open the window of the little house lines up perfectly with the staircase, the wall behind painted, incidentally, in bright magnolia. Watson, be good enough to recite your pocket book list.”

I coughed importantly, and did as asked:

“Two child's three-legged stools, curtains, one teddy bear, one clear glass paperweight, three dolls, one table, one small lamp with thick pebble lens ...”

“That will do,” directed my colleague, accepting another sandwich. “I trust, at last, the matter is resolved, you all comprehend?”

I confess, Mrs Normanton, Mary and myself were stumped. We looked blankly ahead. What on earth was he driving at? We were at a total loss trying to make something of it and failing.

“You're a trifle quick off the mark, Holmes,” I suggested heatedly, somewhat peeved. “Be good enough to expand upon your deductive reasoning; we are not all of us geniuses, blessed with your turn of mind.”

“Forgive me, I shall repeat myself: The Lantern Slide Principle. I say again, my dear Mrs Normanton. Now I shall elaborate further. Your page simply located a photographic glass plate showing your uncle, painted, that is matted out the background, leaving only the old gentleman's image. Thus hidden, kneeling in the toy house, projected by means of the pebble lens lamp and clear glass paperweight a much magnified, startling, life-like semblance of Dunbridge Spettisberg onto the far wall beside the staircase. Timed to perfection, it was your husband's misfortune when leaving the study to, say, fetch a cigar from the box here on the table, to fleetingly encounter this so-called 'ghost' of your relative and thence suffer a confounded shock of nerves. Tommy, I hasten to add, acted in conjunction with those on the outside. He was able to duplicate the key to the safe by means of a wax impression, the work then being carried out by others. He should have quickly rid himself of the stolen ruby brooch by passing it to someone waiting at the kitchen door that same night, who we now know somewhat recklessly threw the empty calf-skin Asprey's case away on the train. An ordinary morning stopping service bustling, crowded with city commuters, calling at Brockley, Honour Oak Park, New Cross Gate and London Bridge, being understood."

"How clever of you, sir, to have fathomed the mystery but, Mary, where is the page? The boy should have been back ages ago."

"Oh, ma'am, he went to post your letters. I can't think where Tommy's got to, he's normally so punctilious."

"Your page," said Holmes, pursuing his thin lips in disdain, "will, I fear, never return to take up his duties. You will recall earlier, madam, when we first arrived you introduced me as 'Mr Sherlock Holmes'. As a miscreant, even so young, well-versed in criminality, he would have heard that name before and understood, with certain trepidation, I am a consulting detective with a successful record of arrests and convictions. But to continue, I am intrigued to know the name of the solicitor who first contacted you regarding the last will and testament, who presumably should have been party to the long list of valuable or worthless artefacts in his client's possession. This Asprey's ruby brooch, the heirloom, Robespierre's guillotined skull, the Poe manuscript and so forth come to mind."

"Why, Mr Holmes, a Mr Edward Lambart."

"Might I enquire whether you have encountered recently any disabled persons, new to the neighbourhood like yourselves?"

"Why certainly – dear Miss Archer and her sister Constance – we invited them for lunch occasionally."

"Wheeled chairs?"

"Bath chairs, ladies' invalid carriages, as such fangled machinery is referred to."

"Oh, ma'am," exclaimed Mary, who had been retained having been in service with Mrs Normanton's late uncle. "I alus recall at the end of every month, t'was the master's custom to slip up to the East End, for he visited a curio shop in Horditch run by a very, very old man, a Mr Isiah Greggs, what was a respectable dealer and sold him all that junk he was so addicted to collecting. I believe Mr Spettisberg visited the solicitor at his office who advised him from time to time."

"Let us altogether dispense with the hypothetical – my own view is that this old, old man, Mr Greggs, is, in fact, 'a fence'. Forgive me, Mrs Normanton, a cockney slang, a person who receives stolen goods and then sells them on at immense profit. Proposing himself as an antiquarian's best friend, Mr Greggs, no doubt, in appearance, a kindly, conscientious elderly expert to be wholly trusted, having accumulated decades of knowledge concerning curios and antiques of every description, gathering a rosta of gullible customers, enticing them to part with their money."

"The ruby brooch was already stolen, you infer, Mr Holmes. It is mine illegally?"

"Precisely. Worth an awful lot of money. The brooch has been unlawfully retrieved from your husband's safe, to place on the market for a second time. Mr Lambart, with his inside knowledge, the brains behind robbing your house, your page presumably being a recent addition to your household staff?"

"Tommy was taken on and interviewed but a month past, it is true. Am I now to understand the precious heirloom is no longer an heirloom? Mine to pass on to my girls Zita and Illumina?"

"My dear Mrs Normanton, if I and Dr Watson were to retrieve the brooch it would solely be police property. Your dear disabled friends, the sisters, will, I believe, also disappear from the scene, for their characters are entirely fabricated. Most likely female impersonators."

"Oh, it's all so silly," said the dear lady with a sigh. "I'm going to make a bonfire of most of uncle's things anyhow. They just clutter the place so."

"By the by, Robespierre's skull, the artefact you mentioned on the train, Mrs Normanton, unique for the clearly defined fracture upon the jawbone, the crack where, in life, the betrayed French revolutionary leader was shot by a pistol ball when being arrested and spent his last days in agony as a consequence, has, I perceive, been swapped by a death's head of far more common provenance, lacking any scar to the jaw. I noticed this up in the attic earlier."

"How unusual, how absurd, Mr Holmes. I myself handled Robespierre's skull when I first came to the house, and witnessed the fracture first hand. I ask you, gentlemen, can that horrid thing actually be of any value to anyone?"

4

Returning to our digs in Baker Street, Holmes having stopped off at the postal telegraphic office to send a wire informing Inspector Lestrade at Scotland Yard of his concerns regarding a Mr Greggs' curio shop in the East End, most likely a hub for receiving stolen goods, additionally impressing upon his old sparring partner the need for more consistency, a greater police response, when in pursuit of apprehending Edward Lambart.

We thus arrived at our rooms to find an envelope upon the mantelshelf containing an official invitation, no less, from Sir Oliver Lodge to attend the Scarborough Psychical Society conference taking place that weekend. It must be said, that evening I caught the first signs of a black mood developing, this Edward Lambart, or rather the solicitor's continued avoidance of the law, beginning to cause incessant brooding, a tendency for morbid introspection.

Returning by train from Brockley, my colleague talked of nothing save Lambart, his mind, I knew, becoming dangerously obsessed, for he had undoubtedly been the mastermind behind the ruby brooch theft and succeeded.

"Scarborough will do us good," said I. "A weekend away from London is long overdue."

"Lambart," he groaned, tumbling into his fireside chair, appearing despondent. "Lambart."

"Stop this," I insisted. "You morbidly excite yourself, Holmes. I need not remind you, Sir Oliver Lodge is a much respected personage. He is at the helm of the research society. To ignore this invitation is to insult a man of great integrity. I insist we pack this instance. Cannot you shift yourself to check the Bradshaw, stay your inclination to brood for long periods. Dammit all, the Northern Express, I recall, has a first-rate Pullman dining car. If we move ourselves now we should be in good time to catch the train."

———

Concerning that most interesting of spa towns, groups of established houses rising in tiers above the recess of a fine, open bay along the coast by the North Sea, Robin Hood Bay in one direction, Bridlington the other, the terraced promenade, the castle one hundred feet above the sands, amongst the resort's popular attractions is the Scarborough Theatre that puts on a varied programme throughout the year.

Travelling on our train, rattling from York along north-eastern main line metals, our compartment shared with a group of actors, we were informed by the guard that many carriages were packed with lady suffragettes amassed in great number to attend the opening night of a new play, Ladies First, of which I, and Mr Sherlock Holmes, being so busy, had apparently overlooked until one of the actors present pointed out the play, in three acts, portended the introduction of membership for two women into the all-male preserve of a distinguished London club in Pall Mall, and there was much debate – letters to The Times, and so forth, damning such ridiculous presumptions on the part of its playwright Stan Hayden, himself a native of Scarborough.

The very concept was nonsense, of course. No women should ever get near any of the top London clubs: White's, The Reform, The Diogenes, The Athenium, The Savage – all were solely a male preserve and would always remain so. Patently, the playwright was courting controversy merely for the sake of securing a West End opening.

The next day, having been recommended first rate accommodation at the Bull Inn, the conference being held that weekend at the Royal Hotel, after consuming a hearty breakfast of kippers, saw Holmes and myself taking a leisurely stroll down by the harbour. The weather, as befits November, was cold and stormy. The front pages of both The Times and Telegraph that morning devoted column inches to the arrest of Edward Lambart and the raiding by police of an antiques shop in Horditch, Inspector Lestrade in charge. Both Greggs and the solicitor were on remand at an East End police station and this pleased my esteemed colleague no end.

Earlier, we had noticed about the resort an influx of boisterous ladies – more train loads, contingents of suffragettes brandishing placards such as 'We believe in Ladies First', 'Hooray – Ladies First the Vote', 'Ladies First Equal Rights', 'Ladies First allowed membership to Brookes and the Reform'."

The first night performance at the Scarborough Theatre was sold out, receiving untold publicity due to the controversial theme – newspapers were full of scathing criticism and praise – a West End opening assured.

We lunched back at the Bull Inn and were seated in the conference room of the Royal Hotel by two o'clock. Sir Oliver Lodge, after greeting the audience, introduced the first speaker to broach psychical matters, a genuine, properly documented case of haunting. A Mr Whaley, a resident of Whitby and member of a séance group who was himself employed as a fitter working on the railway, began his recital, his lecture proving most interesting, holding my attention throughout:

"Whitby Station, gentlemen, the Locomotive Works is responsible for maintaining many steam engines. My account, however, concerns one particular locomotive. It was optimistically aimed to overhaul the loco to pristine condition ready for the following summer.

"Over the winter months, however, a number of queer accidents occurred and the men were becoming increasingly wary about the major overhaul of this locomotive. One had even gone so far as to complain to the works manager of the increasing aura of menace and ill luck that seemed to blight the old Yorkshire engine.

"But something stranger still was brought to the attention of the works manager, Mr Mitchell, by the night shift superintendent. 'I just don't understand this, Mr Mitchell. Can components really be vanishing? The double dome, buffer beam and coupling were as good as gleaming. None of the staff have worked on the locomotive since we attached chains and barely finished overhauling the boiler.' The works manager had some interesting observations of his own. 'Bert, do you recall that nasty dent along the side of the smokebox?' 'I do, Mr Mitchell.' 'This sounds fantastic I know, but young Jenks, the panel beater, one of the best we've got, swears the metal's somehow expanded and sprung back worse than before. By the way, poor old Sands got his fingers badly pulped the other morning when he was riveting the retaining bars across the droplights.'

"But the next day brought further calamity. Mr Nedlow fell off the cab roof and hurt his arm – while he lay on the workshop floor, the senior fitter is reported to have heard mocking laughter emanating from the boiler of the locomotive.

"Witnesses backed him up and tools were downed, staff refusing to continue with the overhaul. A crisis meeting was convened for Sunday at seven o'clock in the office of Whitby Works. Engine drivers, fitters, paint shop boys, machinists, engineers were present. The atmosphere was expectant.

"On everyone's mind was how quickly the spooky locomotive could be cut up and sold for scrap – that seemed the wisest course. No one wanted to go near that shed anymore.

"To the surprise of many in the room, the works manager, Mr Mitchell, introduced a local clergyman – the Reverend Percy Cork, a lifelong Yorkshire railway buff, respected railway historian and author of several good books. He peered at the assembled rabble through a smog of pipe and cigarette smoke and, choking into his handkerchief, opened the meeting with a pertinent question: 'Is it scientifically or metaphysically feasible for a steam locomotive to become the catalyst for evil?'

"A hand shot into the air. 'Engines on the Whitby to Pickering branch undoubtedly have their own distinctive characters,' Mr Rodney, one of the drivers piped up. 'But they are, what I should basically call, "Good old types".'"

I recall vividly how everyone shifted round on their hardback chairs. So – if we are each of us to be persuaded that it is perfectly feasible for a locomotive to have, what we might call, a 'friendly spirit' – could it also be equally possible for it to be malevolent?

The waiting room became hushed and the tobacco smoke seemed to intensify as Mr Whaley hastened to pass around a report.

ENGINE – YORKSHIRE: CLASS NO. 32440 – a catalogue of disasters by the Very Rev. Percy Cork, M.A., Whitby – 7 August 1879: Engine in collision. Mr Nettles blamed for driver error, but denies negligence. Never fully recovered – committed suicide later that year.

WHITBY – 6 June 1876 – Engine ran into buffers crushing flagman. Brake failure initially blamed, but later inspection reveals them to be in perfect working order.

GROSMONT – 23 December 1892 – Engine involved in collision with passenger service on down main line – fatalities – many injured. Sid Marsden blamed for driver error but denies negligence; claims there is a cover-up. Commits suicide exactly one year to the day on anniversary of crash.

PICKERING – 6 February 1888 – Engine abruptly mounted platform with wholesale destruction of ticket office. Investigators could find no mechanical fault.

The audience were in two minds. My colleague, first to raise his hand, mirrored this undercurrent of feeling in the room.

"Alas, Mr Whaley, I must question the authenticity of your account. Is this, in fact, a first- rate example of workers on the make? A clear attempt to convince management that an entire locomotive should be cut up for scrap metal value – the men pocketing the proceeds – I think that ..."

My colleague was interrupted in mid flow. The secretary discreetly directed Sherlock Holmes and I to reception, for an Inspector Ramsden of Yorkshire Constabulary was waiting.

"My dear Inspector Ramsden, I well recall our time spent in Haworth unravelling 'A Village Conspiracy', your Yorkshire force exemplary. Pray, you appear overwrought – evidently you are concerned with a case of some merit requiring my assistance as a consulting detective. We are comfortably ensconced, by the way, in a spacious boarding house establishment on the cliff."

My colleague, sat in a lounge chair, lit his briar- root pipe, listening with interest as Ramsden expounded on the purpose of his visit. "Thou's got it in one, Mr Holmes. A body has come to our attention, discovered inside one of them bathing machines popular round 'ere in summer. It's out a mystery. A small contusion on the lower lip. No marks of violence, nay struggle, fully clothed, even got ee's 'at still in place. But the question remains, 'ow did 'e get there, that's downright queer. The yonder bathing machine is nowt to do wi' 'im."

"No simple case of a vagrant, a tramp loitering, camping down ..."

"Right again, Mr Holmes. T'corpse is summat of a celebrity, mind – a Scarborough chappie, local playwright name of Stan Hayden, who should have by rights turned oop fer't rehearsals this afternoon, but were absent. An' we now know why."

"I recognise the name."

"Ladies First, the play he wrote, is nationally regarded as a direct affront to men. His detractors must be legion," said I. "Coming up on the train, it was packed with suffragettes who no doubt sympathise with the feminist rallying call of the plot."

Holmes remarked, "I fear Mr Hayden, like so many rising playwrights, failed to grasp the serious nature of controversy. The fellow was ill advised by his agent and now this – most likely murdered; pitiful, but not to be entirely unexpected. Women being allowed membership of a prestigious men's club in Pall Mall is, frankly, overstepping the mark. My brother, Mycroft, should be traumatised."

"Aye, but there's full houses an' talk of t'play opening in London. There was a queue half a mile round't block when I were comin' over 'ere."

Upon arriving by four wheeler, holding on to our hats, Inspector Ramsden, a bluff Yorkshireman if ever, led us across to the windy and drenched beach, buffeted by November gales, a stretch of sand whereon a huddle of redundant bathing machines, best described to the reader as back garden sheds poised upon four enormous wheels, were currently parked up, a Mrs Sharples and her sons responsible for their basic maintenance, ensuring they received a dab of fresh pain every twelve months or so, especially after a winter's exposure to stormy coastal conditions, corrosive salt sea air being endemic.

My colleague, keen to penetrate the mystery of the dead playwright, quickly ascended the timber steps guarded by a number of constables; like myself, at once perceiving the body must have been dragged, fully clothed in a rough twill jacket and old pair of trousers, his footwear removed, into the bathing machine, thence leant against the planking at the back, head slumped forward, a tweed country cap still in place.

Checking the pockets, Holmes put his first query forward to the superintending detective of police. "My dear Ramsden, we find every single pocket barren of personal possessions. Brownish nicotine staining of the deceased's moustache and right forefinger, for example, indicate Mr Hayden was an enthusiastic smoker, like myself, yet no evidence of cigarette tin else matches prerequisite for the addict. Your police, one presumes, have not tampered with the clothing?"

"Certainly not, Mr Holmes. I am a stickler for your advanced methods and ordered everything to be kept just as it were found. Nothing did we either remove or discover in't pockets."

"My dear Watson, Inspector Ramsden, we are posed with an intriguing conundrum. Why did our killer go to such lengths to assiduously empty every pocket? Pray, why also are there no shoes, sandals or other footwear evident on the feet?

The answer is that both the pockets and footwear betray terrible clues that will send the perpetrator of this heinous crime to the gallows." Taking out his magnifying lens, Holmes began an intensive examination that paid immense dividends.

"Observe, by removing a summery cotton sock we can see a blister recently formed upon the heel and instep. By lifting the trouser leg above the knee we are aware of grazing to the back of the calf, the upper thigh, caused, most likely, by Stan Hayden wearing unsuitable socks, the friction in hot weather of restrictive waterproof rubber causing inflammation to the skin. Let us thus safely surmise that, at the time of Mr Hayden's death, he was most assuredly wearing a pair of thigh-length wading boots, for he was but a short distance from the sea. I shall say, with some confidence, the pockets contained bait tins, coiled lengths of fishing twine, a reel also, possibly."

"An angler."

"A night fisherman invited by another to spend many profitable hours along this part of the beach patiently waiting to land sea bass, else prestigious coelacanth plentiful to the coastal waters about Scarborough. Encouraged by stormy weather."

"Thou's to be congratulated. A masterly deduction, but thee 'as yet to propound on how exactly it were done, Mr Holmes. How were Stan Hayden killed?"

"Even as we speak, the murderer lurks close by as it is sometimes common to gloat upon the perceived perfection of his clever handiwork, unable to resist the lure of watching police trying to fathom how murder was done, the body stretchered off the beach, no one the wiser. A kind of inner satisfaction, an evil glow of contempt, a feeling of superiority over his fellow man convinces our 'gloater' he will never be caught, that he has committed the perfect crime. Alas, he fails to take into account the involvement of a consulting detective who seeks, and indeed will upon this occasion, outwit him.

"Gather at the top of the steps of the lady bathers' machine, take the greatest care not to betray our interest. My dear Watson, Inspector, please be good enough to notice at some distance along the sands an angler arrived only a short time after us to begin his night watch and assemble his camp: collapsible stool, canvas and post tent, lantern, bait box, insulated flask for soup, or some such, the bendy sea fishing rod balanced on a sturdy support, the long line stretching out to sea. The angler wants for nothing but to hook his first fish. But last night mischief was abroad, for while Stan Hayden sat a little way back, no care of imminent danger, every bit the contented angler, his companion quite abruptly, by the expert casting of his line by means of flicking the rod effecting a whiplash, the fly hook perfectly flew back, attaching itself to the playwright's lower lip, hence the bruising and contusion. Trying to extract the barb, Hayden unwittingly hastened his own end for it was coated in a deadly poison that your police pathologist shall concur under stringent laboratory tests."

"The scoundrel," said I.

"We, the Yorkshire Constabulary, must arrest him at once, Mr Holmes."

"Too prompt, Ramsden, and he may yet cut his own throat; maintain the illusion. The body is removed; thereafter, your men return disguised as happy anglers fishing for bass else coelacanth, then they pounce and restrain the individual, a Black Maria close to hand. Oh, by the by, might I present you both with a somewhat crumpled, coffee-stained copy of last Thursday's Scarborough Gazette. I have ringed a small piece from the celebrity column. A disgruntled thespian:

Top Yorkshire actor, Len Cottingham, saddened that the part of Lord Rill, the membership secretary of the prestigious Pall Mall Gentlemen's Club in the play Ladies First, in a surprise move has been offered to Terry Cruft, the popular West End star, said: 'I knew nothing about it. I had been in rehearsals for the play here at the Scarborough Theatre when I was told the news by the props man. Stan and I remain the best of friends and I wish him every success with the first night performance.'

5

On the Monday we took our seats, comfortably ensconced in a first-class railway compartment of a Pullman express bound for York and London. Holmes, ebullient over his having assisted our dear chum, Inspector Ramsden of the Yorkshire Constabulary, to bag both a chilling and remarkably original killer, the disgruntled actor, Len Cottingham, who, later in police custody, admitted to murdering his professional acquaintance, the northern playwright Stan Hayden, along the sands while night fishing over the matter of his dismissal from the play, treated disgracefully, told to leave the production without proper notification; Hayden, complicit in engaging the West End star, Terry Cruft, despite the Yorkshire actor's previous agreement to play the part, he already having rehearsed the character of Lord Rill for a month or more. The play itself, Ladies First, everyone in the cast were agreed, would become a smash West End box office hit.

Whilst Holmes lit his pipe with a vesta, a lingering fug of smoke beholden to the strongest shag tobacco, filling my own pipe with 'Ships' mixture, I was about to consider the cricket scores, to open my Daily Telegraph at the relevant page, when my eye happened to glance over the most atrocious headlines.

LAMBART ESCAPES

East End solicitor, on remand for masterminding a number of criminal enterprises, including the Hackney jewel theft, was last night reported 'on the run', having by means of a disguise fled the police station where he and a fellow crook, a Mr Greggs, were being kept until Monday. Although clever at outwitting the police, Edward Lambart is not thought to be any danger to the public at large.

Being a through-corridor train, a kindly, elderly vicar, together with a pair of old ladies, took their seats in our compartment, likewise reading their newspapers else glancing out of the carriage window at the passing scene, the spa town retreating into the distance, the day bitterly cold, dismal and overcast. Throughout the remainder of the journey, keeping mostly to ourselves, spending a long lunchtime in the luxury of the Pullman dining car, I confess I paid little heed to our fellow passengers who were, for the most part, lost in perusing novels, one I happened to notice – Thelma by Marie Corelli. As is often the case, however, as we came nearer to the foggy capital, the London terminus, a greater intimacy developed. Our conversation had drifted toward Africa. "I do so applaud all the hard work put in by our nuns and young doctors at the African missions, Reverend Alford."

The vicar nodded. "The continent be so vast, my dear Mrs Worthy, the heat, the dusty roads, want for water holes; why, to traverse from one village to the next must involve many miles requiring much patience and fortitude, but the Lord's will be done. Oh, I will have a boiled humbug, perhaps these gentlemen may like to sample your delicious confections, Mrs Chaste."

"Oh, would you, sirs? The boiled sweets are, I fear, much depleted, but please help yourselves from the remainder in the bag. Humbugs are so refreshing. Pass the bag to the gentleman in the corner, Dorothy, don't hog them so."

I reached out and dipped into the bag. "Thank you," said I, seeing with amusement Sherlock Holmes, more out of politeness than want, not wishing to cause the old ladies undue offence, popping one into his mouth also.

Instantly, a change in my perception took place. Unaccountably, I began to feel a wave of nausea, my vision doubled for a time. I felt myself as though floating off the cloth-covered compartment seat. Once I was more stable, it did not take me long to realise, with a growing feeling of dread, that I was incapable of moving a muscle, that I had been effectively paralysed on the express to London, as indeed had my colleague.

Swiftly removing their female disguises, pawing at the putty layers of stiff make-up on their faces, removing wigs, false eyebrows, Jack Cawdaw and Troughton emerged triumphal, presenting a terribly menacing aspect, giving each of us a hate-fuelled, resentful stare in turn.

The friendly vicar, now of course revealed as none other than Edward Lambart who should have, by rights, been under lock and key, spat out the words,

"Wheeled chairs – you remembered. Luggage vans –
one for each of 'em."

"You are conversant with the occult, I trust?" asked
the solicitor at length, settling once more on his seat.
"The power of séance; I have, myself, spent many
years, Mr Holmes, Dr Watson, gaining valuable
knowledge and experience from such mediumistical
luminaries as the séance society leader, Major
Churchward, who tours Great Britain from time to
time. Of course, you cannot reply, neither of you is
presently capable of speech, but you can hear and see
perfectly well, the drug absorbed into the sweets we
used most effectively to paralyse your body; but I
hasten to say, not your clever, receptive minds.
Robespierre's skull, once the property of my late
client, the antiquarian Dunbridge Spettisberg of
Brockley, Major Churchward assured me I should
forthwith obtain by any means, for by possessing the
Frenchman's distinctive skull we might, if the Major
succeeded in doing so, raise the spirit of Robespierre
himself, and be guided by his wealth of experience.
Before being executed in Paris, he was a formidable
force in politics, both cruel and calculating, sending
thousands to the guillotine. By means of the upturned

glass the alphabet cards we are able to understand Monsieur Robespierre perfectly, and fully prepared to implement strict directives so that he can become energised, fully fleshed to walk amongst us once more. I grant you, blood must be spilled, and I have already, thanks to my friends Jack Cawdaw and Troughton, acquired a most suitable sacrificial lamb. You, my dear Holmes and Watson, shall be, later, witness to the stupendous transition of Monsieur Robespierre from a spirit form to something more substantial. How fortunate that providence retained the skull, the Frenchman's personality, always superlatively evil and arrogant, preserved within the cranium."

"What a clever man you are, Lambart," said my colleague nonchalantly, stirring in his seat, far from being drugged – brightly alert, fully functional; withdrawing a revolver from his inner pocket, he waved it in the crooks' direction. "A séance enthusiast indeed, an occult worshipper. I'm glad you have an engaging hobby," Holmes sneered. "Before I blow your brains out, allow me to fling wide the compartment door. I, as a rule, abhor boiled humbugs, so sticky and sugary in flavour. As a consequence, unlike my friend Watson here, I neglected to properly place one in my mouth. Very good to make your acquaintance, Mr Lambart, in the guise of the friendly vicar, The Reverend Alford, so full of zeal. I myself favour the garb of the cloth for disguise purposes."

Wagging his loaded firearm toward the breezy exit, the swiftly passing 'up line', the rushing telegraph poles, the trees whizzing past, Holmes reiterated his position. "Now, perhaps if you would care to step outside, I'm an amenable fellow, the train does appear to be slowing down along the embankment, the weather rather damp and chill, but that is to be expected in November. Get out I say, the three of you. No doubt you are aware Scotland Yard shall not hesitate to take my side, supportive of my actions in a court of law. Provocation by known criminals, one of them recently escaping remand more than enough reason for me to finish you off."

"You swine, Holmes, you've not heard the last of me," cried Edward Lambart, his hair blown about, clothes flapping in the rushing air, prepared, like the other two, to take a chance and leap out of the moving carriage, no engine apparently due in the other direction, a chance, at least, of escaping with their lives.

"You owe us," was the last response I heard as the criminals tumbled out of the open door one by one, my colleague, using all his considerable strength to slam it shut against the vacuum of breeze as our train rattled along. I observed, from my altered state, my companion reach up for my Gladstone medical bag and, in a thrice, produce a short syringe and bottle that I knew as a doctor contained a shot of vitamin supplement, to stave off the worst effects of the debilitating drug I had unwittingly consumed into my bloodstream. By the time we attained Paddington, although feeling a trifle light-headed, I had regained all movement and was passably fit and agile.

"Well, Holmes," said I, snatching down my bags, hat and stout ash stick from the luggage rack as we drew into the buffers, "thanks to your not partaking of a boiled sweet we find ourselves clear to take a cab to Baker Street and celebrate a fine victory with Mrs Hudson. I doubt whether our trio of crooks shall be up to much after quitting the train in motion."

My colleague remained cautious and was possessed of other ideas. "I regret to say a celebration is premature, my dear Watson. No sooner are we past concessions, I am to wire Inspector Lestrade at the platform telegraphic office, inform him a 'special' shall be required urgently. The district of Horditch must be arrived at by the quickest means, for Mrs Hudson's life may hang in the balance. I fear she has been kidnapped while performing her tasks at 221B, thrust into the talons of one almost as notorious as Lambart himself. Major Churchward, no less. An occultist, a medium of extraordinary celebrity; a 'sacrificial lamb' was mentioned – we were to be witness to some absurd resurrection process."

"I recall the drift of the conversation, certainly, but whereabouts in Horditch is this letting of blood likely to occur?" I asked as we prepared to clamber out of the stationary express service, steam and smoke engulfing the platform. "Not the mission, the solicitor's office, surely?"

"In reading maps, plans and every document I could muster concerning the rubber works, it came to my attention Kamens, the foulest of factories, has, as its major shareholders, none other than the Churchward family. The Major and his clan mostly own that dratted place, old chap, although I imagine visits the district rarely, perfectly content to accrue shareholder dividends. Major Churchward will be awaiting us and the others, Cawdaw and so forth, to start whatever sacrificial ritualistic preliminaries are required to once more form the tangible figure of Monsieur Robespierre of the Republique, to 'flesh him out', so says the jargon, presumably from that old skull of Mrs Normanton's uncle. We have little time to play our advantage, but Major Churchward will most assuredly be expecting Edward Lambart shortly, and the rest, of course. I believe they would have taken us across London by train anyhow, utilising wheeled chairs, wrapping us in shawls and rugs to thus promote a pair of gaga invalids."

"But you, Holmes, were wholly responsible for scuppering that scurrilous enterprise."

"Precisely. Come, dear boy, the game is afoot. A 'Special' must be commandeered to Horditch."

Lestrade, together with a group of officers, arrived at Paddington terminus in a London growler and from there it was agreed the fastest journey time should be achieved by the specially hired one-coacher. Our engine, unhindered by signals, rattled along foggy viaducts with screaming whistle, subjugated by myriad views of squalor evident from the railway carriage window. Passing Bermondsey Road, Old Street, scene of the wheeled chair mob's almost successful heist on H. Samuels.

Thereby, we achieved our destination, the reader by now much concerned on behalf of our poor landlady, the redoubtable Mrs Hudson, will be asking interminably again and again: were the expedition in fact in time to save her?

For the answer we must bear once more the vile, lingering miasma belching from the chimney of the local rubber factory. One of the premier producers of garden hosepipes for Great Britain and the empire, casting its polluting stench of smoky effluvium in every conceivable nook and cranny of the streets thereabouts. Once gathered in Gasworks Lane, we proceeded past that same place of industry following a length of high wall capped with twisted barbed groups of spikes. The factory gates opened onto a sprawling yard, divided with embedded railway lines criss-crossing the cobblestones.

A group of sheds were being stocked with endless coiled lengths of rubber hosepipe, the tall chimney continued to belch smoke, workmen went about their business. Thus we received no indication whatsoever the exact vicinity Major Churchward intended to conduct occult practices. Our first breakthrough came when enquiring at the works office, an employee mentioned he was certain he had seen Major Churchward arrive in a four-wheeler with others, presumably for a shareholders' meeting.

That was, to Holmes, stretching incredulity. Lestrade, representing the official force, explained we should be conducting a search of the premises for a human skull forthwith. The official, although puzzled, was not averse to our doing so. "Are there perhaps any part of your sheds presently empty and lacking personnel?"

"No. 4, a storage facility, has been closed this last month, for a new arrangement of stacking shelves is being planned and refurbishment imminent. Dear me, Inspector," he chuckled, "a skull you say? I believe there must be a plentiful supply available in churchyards and cemeteries throughout the land. What Kamens Rubber Works should be doing with such a bony and charnel relic I fear is beyond me. But then, I am merely a white-collar worker, a clerk lacking a detective's perception and intelligence." Lestrade did not appreciate this thinly-veiled sarcasm and stumped out of the office, we following.

"Mr Holmes," said he, exasperated, as we strode across the yard heading for the number four storage area, "theorising is all very well, but we, the police, have as yet no sinister occultists in custody, nor this peculiar 'Frenchy' skull – nor have we located your supposedly abducted Mrs Hudson. I trust my time and resources are not being undermined."

"Certainly not," snapped my colleague.

By means of a side entrance, a key supplied by the office clerk earlier, we became introduced to a most gloomy expanse of flooring, the shed heaped with wooden pallets at one end, dominated by long rows of wall shelving. However, the most queer betrayal of a more sinister intent in the midst of innocuous warehouse equipment was a guillotine, accurately constructed, erected upon a plinth, a wickerwork basket horribly evident to catch decapitated heads placed directly beneath the neck brace.

Mrs Hudson sat knitting atop one of the timber steps. She glanced up on hearing our approaching footsteps and, in clear Scotch enunciation, proceeded to inform us of previous events.

"Och, I'll tell you gentlemen how it was. I were kidnapped from 221B and brought here. At around four, Major Churchward and the rest packed up and left. They scarpered for fear of indictment, Mr Holmes. That old skull belonging tae some unpronounceable Frenchman they held so dear started to glow, reminding me I'd tarry of that Edinburgh fancy us girls were partial to a'boot – putting out a lighted lantern from the winda upon a night dogs howled, to keep away the wee evil spirits. It musta communicated something fearful urgent, for they rushed to the séance table, a glass whizzing round, stopping off at alphabet letters. 'Gracious heavens,' cried out Churchward – 'Cawdaw, Troughton and Mr Lambart hae been run down by a north bound express; they are communicating from the other side. Sherlock Holmes outwitted them – the game's up.'"

The skull remained a mystery; despite an extensive search, nowhere to be found.

Major Churchward faced no charges. The grotesque guillotine explained away by managers from the Kamens Rubber Works as simply test apparatus, an innovative means, once steam-belt driven and fully automated, of slicing hosepipe to required lengths; part of our industrial revolution, not the French. From breathing so much bad air emitted by the molten rubber processing, Lestrade, desperate to clear off, had no other course open but to drop the case, for Mrs Hudson, at her time of life, possessed absolutely no interest in pursuing statements, pressing charges and the bother of law courts; she far preferred supervising the decorating of her ground floor apartments which was then in progress at 221B.

The death of Cawdaw, Troughton and Edward Lambart, being run down by an express, according to the papers, along the stretch of track by the cutting approaching Old Oak Common, thankfully brought closure upon months of concern regarding our esteemed Scotch landlady, for which we were immensely relieved.

One wintry night, the lamplighter doing his rounds early, we were honoured to be visited at our digs by none other but the chairman of the Psychical Research Society of London, Sir Oliver Lodge, a stalwart, trimly- bearded fellow of an open countenance with a broad, intelligent brow and piercing blue eyes. He was nattily outfitted in a fur-collared, light grey coat, calf-skin gloves and a satin top hat. Taking the sofa, he expounded upon the reason for his dropping by that evening.

"Mr Holmes, I have a matter of some gravity requiring utter confidentiality. I may say to outsiders – that is unbelievers, those who continue to scoff at, for example, supernormal visitation, spirit possession, I should be regarded by many decent people as somewhat of a batty eccentric."

"My dear Sir Oliver," answered Sherlock Holmes, choosing his favoured long pipe from the rack close by his armchair. "You know me better, surely." He paused to search out his matches. "Whilst I insist upon factual evidence for such phenomena, I am, as is most assuredly Dr Watson, by no means a bigot, remaining keenly open-minded on such controversial issues. Do please continue with your discourse, you have our undivided attention."

"Very well, gentlemen; yesterday morning, it was discovered an extremely rare, thigh-length Parliamentarian boot, in a wonderful state of preservation, had been stolen by thieves from Wigan Museum in Lancashire. This item of footwear, I must emphasise, is unusual in more ways than one, the subject of rigorous tests over a fortnight by two of my most trusted and senior colleagues at the Psychic Society – a Dr Booth and a Mr Cushing. The boot apparently responds to stimuli, and most incredulously of all was able to walk a couple of yards itself. The report states unequivocally that by means of spirit communication, this Parliamentarian boot most certainly once belonged to Matthew Hopkins, the so-called 'witch-finder general' responsible for ducking and hanging women, appointed by Oliver Cromwell to purge the populace of suspected witches."

"Not, I recall, a very savoury character," I remarked with some disgust, cleaning the vulcanite stem of my

'Bent Apple' briar pipe with a goose feather soaked in spirit of meths. "Most modern people today would, frankly, class Hopkins as an out and out sadist, a woman hater. Wasn't he assassinated when his witch hunts got more and more out of control?"

"Yes, he was, by a group of high-ranking Roundheads sworn to secrecy, sick of the whole insane business, the body never recovered, believed to be buried anywhere in England."

"Hopkins aside, pray where was this distinctive Parliamentarian boot discovered?" enquired Holmes, puffing on his pipe, much intrigued, a wreath of blue-tinged smoke clinging about the mantelpiece before rising ceiling-wards.

"By a Mr Renfrew, who lives on a smallholding quite close to an area upon the border of Wigan township referred to as 'Cromwell's Ditch'."

"I see."

"The curator at the Wigan Museum is devastated, Holmes. He cannot comprehend how a thief managed to both retrieve this item of antiquity from its glass display case, nor manage to outwit staff and remove it from the museum altogether without discovery, there being, what, only two small upstairs rooms devoted to smaller items from the local history collection. When I tell you this vintage boot is only one of a few remaining in the country, a genuine artefact that survives from the Civil War period, the leather and metal buckle well preserved – you will understand his obvious concern."

"Thus, your own findings at the Psychical Research Society by these two eminently respectable members prompts you to further pursue the safe retrieval of this object."

"Perfectly correct, Dr Watson. Mr Holmes, it is imperative that Matthew Hopkins' boot be found, this is one of the most startling discoveries, a genuine case of spirit possession that will provide properly documented proof of survival of the human personality after death. I cannot speak plainer."

"Well, Sir Oliver, I shall do my utmost to assist your cause. Fees, expenses must however be met. Naturally, it is the robbery at Wigan Museum that maintains my interest; exactly how the boot was stolen remains an intriguing conundrum."

"My secretary shall be happy to sponsor your trip north, and consequent investigation. I am grateful, Mr

Holmes, to have ascertained your services as a most unique consulting detective."

Once more we took the express north, a most convivial train journey. Alone in our first-class smoking compartment, wine flask and a first rate luncheon basket provided, I observed Holmes avidly studying Sir Oliver's Psychic Society report with, I noted, mounting exasperation and scepticism. Eventually he chucked the file over for me to peruse, sneering all the while.

"Piffle, Watson, absolute piffle," said he, settling down to read his copy of the Daily Telegraph, pipe securely poking from the corner of his pursed lips. We smoked and did not talk again for a full hour, by which time I too regarded the findings related by Dr Booth and Mr Cushing as rather suspect.

Wigan is, of course, a flourishing cotton town; it has a chemical works, some twenty large factories abound, a grammar school in Millgate, and much cannel coal is to be mined in the surrounding dales.

The museum, a terracotta and red brick building of similar architectural design to the town hall, displays a strikingly large collection of Civil War period artefacts, a large engraved canon, an imposing waxwork of the great protector himself, Oliver Cromwell.

We were duly received by the curator, a Mr Clough, upon a chilly, dreary morning of continuous rain, the cobbled streets, trod by countless clogs as workers obeyed the call of the factory whistle, awash with a deluge of water, the rain, I confess, never to cease all the while we stayed in Wigan.

Removing our hats and coats we were shown into the curator's office and, over a welcome pot of tea, I recorded in my diary the following conversation, the incessant Lancashire rain hammering against the windowpane all the while.

"I should perhaps, gentlemen, inform you of a little of the history concerning this area," said Mr Clough, lighting a cigarette, leaning back in his chair. "Upon the 25th August 1651, the Earl of Derby, with six hundred horses, was defeated by Colonel Lilburne, a Roundhead. Cromwell, it will be remembered, defeated the Royalist forces in the suburbs of nearby Preston. In Warrington, the Royalist Army, under Lieutenant Bailey, surrendered, prisons of war taken. Cromwell's Ditch is a field on the outskirts of town where the remains of an earthworks, a redoubt, is situated. The great battle of Wigan took place there."

"I recall mention – the Parliamentary boot – your missing artefact was first discovered in that vicinity of the battle," remarked Holmes, lighting his pipe, tossing a spent vesta into the ashtray.

"Just so, Mr Holmes, by a cottager who lives close by. The staff at the museum, the Department of Geology, the local historians, are agreed that the boot was one of a pair belonging to Colonel Ternan, a prominent Roundhead officer under Cromwell killed during the campaign to capture Wigan from Royalist forces. As was customary, high-ranking commanders were buried with due dignity in a proper grave – not a pit."

"But what of this latest report stating the boot in fact belonged to Matthew Hopkins, the notorious 'witch-finder general'? Honestly, Clough, what are your views?" Holmes was himself obviously scathing on the issue.

"Fanciful speculation," the curator replied, shaking his head doubtfully. "These ghost people are always trying to dig out something 'wished for' – sensational. I regard the findings as wholly inaccurate. I'd say speculative. The two gentlemen who carried out the tests under apparently 'the strictest control' conditions were, I'm certain, genuine. Dr Booth and Mr Cushing struck me as both intelligent men, sincere and honourable. I mean, it was I who gave them permission to examine the boot. I certainly don't wish to demean them as people, nor besmirch the reputation of Sir Oliver Lodge, but I just think the idea of a walking boot imbued with the personality of Matthew Hopkins absurd."

"Well," insisted my colleague, in full agreement, "let us lose no time in endeavouring to ascertain exactly how the thief made such an easy conquest of this precious Cromwellian artefact. I confess, your museum here in Wigan seems most secure. The rooms housing the local history collection are where?"

"Upstairs, one flight. Allow me to show the way, gentlemen."

I confess, we spent a remarkably short time actually engaged in assessing the scene. Groups of teak cabinets displaying, behind glass, musket balls, gunpowder pouches, sabres, Roundhead helmets, the odd dagger, were ignored by my esteemed colleague. The empty space where once stood the Cromwellian boot caused a flicker of interest. The floor, however, held him transfixed. Within five minutes, without even employing his trusty tape measure or magnifying glass, Holmes allowed we return forthwith to the curator's office where he would explain his deductions over a pipeful of tobacco.

"I shall begin by referring to the brown lino in the first of the rooms; the well-polished linoleum upstairs bore many round imprints corresponding to the recent pressure of the heel of a very large- sized boot. One does not even require a lens to observe the pressed-in, distinctive marks on the floor, particularly near the cabinet. Does, I wonder,
any member of your museum staff thus wear large boots with tall heels, for instance, a janitor?"

"None of my staff, Mr Holmes," the curator answered promptly, sure of the fact.

"Bravo, well let us now consider another option. Secondly, do you recall a recent paying visitor, say a woman possessed of a notably longer than average skirt?"

"Good gracious, as a matter of fact I do, Mr Holmes. A Mrs Rowls and her husband Vincent, a very nice couple, quite well informed."

"The gentleman, I'll vouch, presenting a bushy beard, prominent eyebrows, wearing, perhaps, a pair of thick-lensed spectacles, pebbly glass, somewhat myopic?"

"Heavens, you have described him exactly. Short-sighted. I can vouch Mr Rowls was squinting at everything. Do go on."

"The Parliamentarian boot upstairs was removed thus: one of these two persons, the gentleman, possessed a wax-impression key to the display cabinet and simply utilised this tried and tested method of obtaining entry. The boot was removed, swiftly placed over the woman's leg beneath her skirts and thus concealed, herself now wearing the Cromwellian footwear, the happy couple waltzed out of the Wigan Museum making their way to the railway station to depart southward. Additionally, your local history section housed upstairs, isolated from the central, more important exhibits concerning the town of Wigan and the natural history of the area on the ground floor should, one presumes, not have been a priority of staffing and little supervised during the morning of the theft, yourself, Mr Clough, no doubt busy in another part of the building. You surely allow people to browse at leisure unattended?"

"A very succinct explanation. The way the boot was stolen, nothing short of remarkable; a wax impression of the key, you say. Well, given the tremendous deception, who were these people – this masquerading couple, Mr Holmes? Have you any idea?"

My companion chose not to be drawn, remaining cautious. "I must, for the time being, keep my council, Mr Clough."

Whilst our train rattled south to the capital, eating dinner in the restaurant car over a bottle of fine burgundy, I presented Holmes with my own analysis. I confess one did not have to delve too deeply to form an opinion upon the Wigan Museum theft, nor have to be a genius to draw certain conclusions.

"Dr Booth and Mr Cushing of the Psychic Society are both in on this – they must be involved," said I, wiping my mouth with a serviette.

"Indeed," agreed Holmes. "Both would surely have easy access to the display cabinet and, during their period of research, ample opportunity to duplicate the key, the obsession with Hopkins being self-evident."

Outside the dining car, many lighted habitations rushed past; a darkening night sky boding yet further rain and gloom. Holmes glanced up from his pheasant and, reposing in his seat, expounded in greater depth. "On the day, have no doubt one of them was dressed as a woman wearing a wig and a long, flowing skirt."

I nodded. "You visited Wigan post office earlier whilst I purchased cigarettes at the tobacconist. Did you perchance send a telegram?"

"No, Watson. I did however manage, by sheer perseverance, to talk a counter clerk into locating in their official directories the address of Dr Booth."

In a rush of smoke, the train blew its whistle and we entered a long stretch of tunnel. "And what is the doctor's address?" I enquired, taking a long draught of wine.

"Number thirty-eight Hob Lane," said he.

"Doesn't the subterranean railway, the station I mean, run along there?" said I.

"Hob Lane is, in fact, in the borough of Horditch upon the other side of the gasworks, deep in the manufacturing heartland of garden hosepipes. The underground steam railway certainly stops there, and by Jove, Watson, that's where we're next headed.

Tonight, however late in the day, I intend to pay a visit to the doctor at number thirty- eight, making relevant enquiries about a specific Cromwellian leather boot missing, believed stolen. Now, dear fellow, I insist, before our foray takes us once more into the filth and degradation of Horditch, you concentrate upon demolishing that most excellent and delicious of roast fowl set before you. Another hour or so and we shall have attained the London terminus."

7

"'Ob Lane, 'Orditch – you aint' serious -you'se pullin' me leg; you ain't goin' there at this time of night, is you gents? I swear it ain't safe for decent citizens like yerselves. Last underground train is due in five minutes – ten to midnight. 'Ang onter yer wallets, an' for gawd's sake, take care."

The porter scowled at our tickets and waved us through the barrier. "You is armed, I trust," he added, seriously. "Wheeled chair mob rules the roost in that part of Lunnon. Me and the missus avoids the shops if we can 'elp it. They ain't afraid to use shooters, neiver." He shook his head in disbelief at such perceived folly and began preparing for the incoming train.

The underground was hot and sulphurous. A fug of unventilated locomotive smoke hung about the platform and tunnels. My hair and clothes were already covered in coal smuts. I perceived we were the only passengers travelling on the line at that late hour. The whole subterranean network seemed to me both claustrophobic and unnerving. A locomotive soon shunted into the platform.

Once we had achieved Hob Lane underground station, bracing ourselves against the chill, clammy fog existing above ground, that and the ever- present odour of molten rubber being processed all night by Kamens, it did not take us long to locate the address. But we were in for a surprise, for number thirty-eight was, in fact, a doss house, a workhouse, a plain, functional building set back from the pavement. Originally instituted by the Poor Law Board guardians, these grim barracks were conceived to combat pauperism, more recently to shelter down-and-outs, providing a monotonous regime of work, regular meals and a place to bed down.

The frosted glass windows at the front of this bleak edifice were barred and secure. Light blurred by the creeping fog blanketing the street shone dimly from within, indicating someone was up and about at least. My companion directed we avoid knocking up the workhouse supervisor, so alternatively we headed round the side of the building, encountering rows of dustbins. We were in luck! A door was both unlocked and unattended. We slunk through the kitchens dominated by vast cooking vats and ovens and eventually were able to make a brief reconnaissance of certain gloomily lit corridors and wards.

"Dr Booth is no doubt in charge of this place," whispered Holmes, screwing up his beaky nose. "Good Lord, the whiff is severe, Watson."

"Yes, that must be Booth, the medical practitioner's status," I agreed, likewise appalled by the stench of bodies. My skin crawled. Who amongst us with any shred of decency would not recoil at being immersed in such an institutionalised, depressing atmosphere? The row upon row of sleeping dossers like so many corpses. What could be done, I wondered, to counter the hopeless resignation with which these poor wretches accept such a treadmill existence of virtual mental imprisonment day to day; surely society could do better.

Realising I was pontificating, and in reality guilty as everyone else of not giving a damn for the welfare and betterment of such filthy dregs of humanity, I followed Holmes through swing doors whereupon we found ourselves in what was recognisably the infirmary.

Shockingly, the beds were occupied by a group of obviously lobotomised inmates, electrodes sporting short lengths of copper wire attached to the cranium of each individual. None stirred, mouths agape. Sedated, these shrouded shapes might just as well have been corpses, yet despite this – how, I know not – the copper wire implants fizzed and emitted blue flame. I heard groaning, the inmates sensing our presence, which I confess unnerved me. I observed the lights from the gas jets fluctuated, the gloom intensified. The beds and their lumpen, prone occupants staring at us fell further into shadow, the copper wires occasionally sparking briefly.

"'Elp me, sirs," gasped one of them, a man not yet shaven headed, moving his bony fingers weakly, beckoning us come hither to the iron bedstead he occupied.

I observed a poor old fellow whom I judged to be well into his eighties, feeble, bedraggled and utterly wretched, wearing a hospital smock. "Name's Toddy Price," he wheezed. "Boof ain't finished wiv me yet, sirs, but 'e's done wiv Alfie Bates, Charlie 'Erbert an' the uvvers. Operatedon their skulls, some'ow bleedin' fiddlin' around inside their 'eads. The bastard wants six of us fer a big séance over at the rubber works. I'm 'earin' we've bin converted to be useful, productive, like. 'Ow, I don't understand. Why 'e fitted electrodes an' copper wire is beyond me."

"Kamens," I ejaculated.

"Just so; a fella called Churchward is co- ordinatin' the meetin', 'im an' some fiend in a wheeled chair. 'E visited the infirmary on Wednesday – nasty, disabled type, eyes like a reptile's. Gawd, I'm scared. 'Elp me, 'elp me, guv."

"Calm yourself, Mr Price."

"Well, see, I'm 'avin' an op tomorrow, then I'll be jest like the rest in 'ere, more dead than alive. You got a gun to finish me orf, guvnor?"

"My dear fellow, your mental anguish is perfectly understandable; however, the puzzle remains – why on earth are these electrodes implanted into their scalps? For what purpose the two copper wires protruding from the top of the head? Why are five inmates being systematically lobotomised?" Desperate for answers. Holmes was barely able to contain his mounting annoyance at being unable to fully comprehend.

"I told yer, guv, a big séance 'do'; special like, over at the factory. We're summunk to do wiv that. Participants," he croaked.

"When?" asked my colleague, eagerly.

"Tomorrer night – Saturday, I fink. Look, I'se don't know no more, okay? You'd best scat, gents. The doc's sure to be checkin' us up later. Take my tip and gerrout o' 'ere fast." The poor chap with his weakened constitution soon relapsed back into unconsciousness. The gas jets secured to the wall flared briefly.

I confess, about all I could do at that stage was tuck in the sheet, plump the dosser's pillow and wish Mr Price luck, yet the information he imparted was to prove of crucial significance.

Suddenly, we became aware of distant taps, rapidly approaching footsteps along the corridor. Making haste to escape the way we had come, locating the kitchens we exited along the side alley cluttered with dustbins, back onto Hob Lane whereupon, after a long walk, reaching the outskirts of Horditch, we were able to summon a cab and head across London to Baker Street.

————

After bath and bed we awoke suitably refreshed, prepared to tuck into an ample breakfast of curried chicken and ham and egg prepared by our landlady Mrs Hudson, who had that morning laid table and given the coal fire a stout poke to liven it up.

Our front sitting room remained warm and cosy although outside, the ochre fog still lay thick about the metropolis, the dun-coloured houses opposite barely perceived, the normally persistent clatter of horse buses, delivery carts and hansoms somewhat muffled.

"I had a dashed queer dream last night, Watson," said my friend, peering over the silver-plated coffee pot with a fulsome appetite, choosing one of the heated dishes from which to heap up his plate. I poured coffee for both of us and sympathised.

"Really, old chap," said I. "That dreary workhouse infirmary is enough to give anybody convulsions and nightmares for a week at least. Well, go on."

"The words 'you owe us', should be enough of a clue," he laughed, "demands for ransom, back pay — remind you of someone?"

"Oh, that trio of scoundrels. Presumably the ex-Baker Street Irregular. The late Jack Cawdaw making a show, sporting that awfully loud canary- yellow, checked suit of his, and that equally obnoxious lilac bowler. A nightmare indeed."

"Indeed, comparable to a visitation from the other side of the veil. I dreamt I was on trial for my life, believe it or not, at the Horditch rubber works – in that vast warehouse. My judge was Robespierre's vindictive skull, grinning, glowing furiously, hovering in mid-air. The three of our antagonists appeared morose, seething for revenge. Troughton and Lambart were not exactly happy about being mown down by a train, an oncoming express, their spirits perturbed, resentful."

"That's entirely their own stupid fault." I was adamant. "If, when alive, they'd jumped out of the open compartment door of the moving train when you suggested, Holmes, that being when we reduced speed along by the embankment, they might have stood a chance ... might have." I continued to attack my meal with gusto. "So, we're back to that Frenchie's fractured skull, are we? Like Matthew Hopkins, Robespierre was of warped intelligence, a truly evil blighter. He sent thousands to the guillotine, presiding over many executions in Paris, watching gleefully as the tumbrils arrived. I mean, Holmes, it's startling. Look what we've uncovered so far, all in consequence of a cracked skull and a missing Cromwellian boot. Mrs Hudson kidnapped, found at the foot of a lethal guillotine explained away by the Kamens managers who twisted every argument in their favour and got Churchward off the hook. And now we've got that poor old dosser Toddy Price to answer to. Can't we lay siege to the Hob Lane workhouse and mount a daring rescue, Lestrade or Bradstreet at the helm? Involve Scotland Yard once again? At least save Toddy, our old vagrant from being experimented on and wired up."

"Way too late," my colleague said caustically, totally dismissive of my proposal. "Our best way forward, Watson, is to turn up at the factory this Saturday evening and find out what the devil that séance is all about. After all, our dosser provided us with valuable data; the least we can do is take advantage of the intelligence Mr Price provided."

"I suppose so," said I, "although it sounds a bit crass and heartless the way you put things, Holmes." My companion reached over for the cut- glass marmalade pot and grinned.

"You know, Watson, I'm rather looking forward to our next foray into Horditch tonight. Why, I'm starting to miss that toxic smell of processed rubber already." He chuckled. "Aren't you, dear boy – are you not perhaps becoming a teeny weeny bit addicted?"

"Certainly not," I blustered, believing his jokey aside to be in very poor taste, not daring to contemplate Toddy Price's awful fate, hoping that somehow we would save him.

————

That same evening, joining others shovelling coke into a bunker over by the furnace house, from what we could gather, the lobotomised dossers from Hob Lane workhouse had been transported covertly across Horditch by Kamens delivery carts, and once through the factory gates and in the cobbled yard were led inside the warehouse in pairs. Poor Toddy, I noted with revulsion, now bald, his skull like the rest, having been opened up. I cringed when I spied a pair of electrodes, glinting under the glow from a gas mantle, implanted in the poor old fellow's cranium. How on earth someone of that advanced age actually survived such an invasive surgery beggared belief, but here he was, wearing the same hospital smock, gazing blankly ahead, shuffling along hand in hand, paired with another inmate, one of his infirmary kin. Did, I wonder, Mr Price know, did he realise, was Toddy in any way aware of what was happening to him? I hoped in heaven's name not; however, the core reason for these poor wretches being implanted with copper wiring eluded us still.

I should emphasise both Holmes and myself were, at this juncture, disguised as workers, long- serving rough types, loyal to Kamens, my colleague having on our last visit made an intricate study of the garments worn by employees of the rubber processing plant: navy blue overalls and steel toe-capped, hobnail boots which we accordingly adopted; also, cloth caps and wide leather belts were de rigueur. Droopy moustaches, Piccadilly whiskers, a pastel blend of green and yellow shades of skin colour, both sickly and ghoulish, gave the excellent effect of long-term pollution poisoning after so many years working in such close proximity to the furnace house.

I can report Holmes' genius for making up was undiminished and not one person bothered to question our movements. Indeed, we even brazenly took a mug of tea and plate of egg and chips in the subsidised canteen without raising an eyebrow. I cheerfully once more slipped into my cockney persona; borrowed coils of garden hosepipe slung over our shoulders, and a spittle- stained roll-up drooping from the corner of our mouths completed the pretence.

At half past seven, Holmes pointed out carriages had arrived and parked in the yard. Sure enough, that bounder Major Churchward, looking very pleased with life, entered the warehouse complex accompanied by a number of disabled chaps in wheeled chairs. Here was our call to action. Losing no time, we hurried through a side entrance and a while later, before the doors were locked, managed to discreetly penetrate the séance meeting.

I cannot adequately convey the absolute horror of the scene that awaited us – the séance was about to progress, all was in place. A massive, polished, oval table was central; sat round this were eight to ten participants, fingers placed upon a large, upturned tumbler. But the six dossers were additional company; each stooped over, bent down, the top of their heads wired into terminals at the table's edge. Cable led from them to a large, bulky generator, an electricity accumulator, fan- belt driven, from above.

"Robespierre, are you with us?" The skull in the centre of the table rose into the air and nodded. "Then let us begin transfiguration. The whole process should take little more that five minutes. Gentlemen, please put on the special dark-lensed rubber goggles provided, which shall protect us against the glare of harmful rays. Those in wheeled chairs please cover your lower extremities with the rubber sheets provided. I need not remind you we are due to raise Matthew Hopkins at ten past eight. As promised, at nine o'clock coffee and biscuits. Before that, however, the ladies who you are all dying to meet, our special, regenerated guests, shall be next materialised once our master, Robespierre, is fully fleshed and again safely among us. Keep your attention always focused upon the upturned tumbler. Pay no heed to the smell of singed, else burnt, flesh. This need not distract us. Dr Booth will verify the purpose of the Hob Lane inmates plugged into the table is to provide us with a surge of human energy and each dosser is expendable once the process is wrought."

Major Churchward, a top medium and psychic directing proceedings, nodded to an operator stood over by an ugly black box on casters that must, in my estimation, have weighed a ton at least. The ugly metal contraption hummed continuously. He threw a number of switches, dials flickered. Hunched over, almost bent double, spaced round the table, the half dozen inmates from Hob Lane infirmary, supervised by Dr Booth, began to vibrate, their curved spines quiver and undulate. The men's bald heads wired into the table glowed perceptively, showers of sparks issuing from their ears and nostrils. Séance members' fingers resting on the upturned tumbler were promptly removed. The glass instantly started to whizz round the entire circumference at incredible speed, so many revolutions per second, leaving a trail of ethereal vapour. Astoundingly, the enormous, king-sized oval table, the actual polished oak furniture, began to light up, emitting a phosphorous green effervescence. The Frenchman's skull with its fractured jaw, meanwhile hovering in the centre, took facial form, fleshing out, revealing a cruel, pinched visage – sharp nose and chiselled chin, a cadaverous, arrogant individual with wild hair clothed in eighteenth-century attire: buckled shoes, knee breeches, torn stockings and a satin shirt with bloody collar. Expressing utter contempt for his captive audience attending the groundbreaking séance to top all séances, he emerged easily recognisable from his waxwork effigy displayed for many years at Madame Tussaud's, rising into the air, floating serenely across before landing steadily upon his feet on the warehouse floor.

Offering a short bow, Robespierre turned to face the major, intoning firmly so that none may doubt his authority what must be done next. "Monsieur Churchward, as we discussed at a previous séance through the planchette, pray proceed avec le programme. Les jeune filles, if you please. Voila, I haff a signal they are ready to breach the veil. Trés bon, pray continue, sil vouz plait."

"Master, I should be honoured," answered the doting sycophant, clearly overcome, marvelling at the successful transfiguration. "You look majestique, Monsieur Robespierre. Bert, pull the switches, if you please. We are, I'm delighted to say, entirely on schedule."

The operator nodded; jerking a lever, the generator once more burst into life, rumbling and emitting a loud hum. Yet again, Holmes and I were witness to an enormous energy surge caused, in part, I surmised, by diverted brainwaves channelled by the group of shaven- headed dossers, who, at this juncture, began to smoulder, their hospital smocks terribly singed. Certain of the inmates rallied, although one of them, unable to stay the course, slumped to the floor, electrodes woefully overheated, bursting into flame, but none participating paid any heed or cared for the dossers' welfare. Instead, while the tumbler whirled constantly round and round the polished table, Churchward suddenly got up, smiling warmly, to address the assembled throng, particularly the tumbler itself in which could be seen reflected five squirming miniature females, inquisitive faces full of wonder and excitement, squashed against the glass. The tumbler slowed down still further until, screeching on the polished surface, it ceased altogether.

"Ladies, may I ask each of you to step forward? Mary Ann Nichol, Annie Chapman, Elizabeth Stride, Catherine Eddoes, Mary Jane Kelly. I bid you welcome to East London, an area you have not lived in nor visited since the year 1888."

Once again applause rang out. One by one, each woman, certain of their number not unattractive, became fleshed out, reaching full height, none, I hasten to add, bearing cut throats or the barbarous mutilations endured at the hands of an unknown slayer of prostitutes, 'Jacky the Terror' or 'Leather Apron' as he was first known. They wore the same costumes associated with the mortuary photographs then widely published: ginger- haired Mary Jane Kelly, the prettiest, a cheeky, chirpy personality, was to be their spokeswoman. She wore a jaunty bonnet, short jacket, hooped stockings, ankle boots and a flouncy frock. She looked quite fetching.

"Monsieur Robespierre," said she, "we thank you for your trust and efforts beyond the veil, and the Major for his earthbound assistance. Hello, East End, we love you. Gawd, it's good to be back." She raised her fist jubilantly in the air; the séance crowd rose from their seats and clapped, the other Whitechapel women clustered in a group grinning hugely.

Bringing calm to the proceedings, Major Churchward, overlooked by a stern and uncompromising Robespierre, began to announce the next item. I confess I heard little of what was said for, by now, Holmes and myself, abandoning the concealment of a stack of pallets, had crept unseen across the floor and were presently crouched behind the black box generator, I busy unscrewing a backplate, Holmes' idea being to make every effort to short-circuit the guts of the thing and cause an electricity explosion. My colleague deftly thrust the metal blade of his pipe knife between the coils of an anemometer, wedging it securely in place before pouring a concoction of lighter fluid and chemicals from his hip flask over the valves in the hope of encouraging extreme malfunction.

"Come, Watson," said he, "we must, I fear, hasten away from the meeting. I'll warrant a warehouse fire of immense destructive power will occur when that operator next pulls the switch."

Sherlock Holmes, choosing his black clay, the filthiest of his pipe collection, filled it with the shag he preferred, his wan, hawk-like features pensive and contemplative.

"Well," said I, slinging him the box of vestas, "what time is Lestrade due?"

"I believe, by the familiar footsteps upon the stair, Watson, Mrs Hudson must have just shown him in." He scratched a match, lit his pipe, puffing out a good deal of smoke that rose ceiling-wards. Shortly after, the ratty-faced Scotland Yarder entered our front sitting room. He appeared out of sorts, pale and worn out. I went over and poured him a cup of reviving coffee from the pot, for which he was grateful.

"What a time I've had of it, Mr Holmes," the detective complained. "Early this morning, I and other officers were sent to deal with a very queer crime, a most puzzling, seemingly motiveless murder of a Mr Ellis who lived quietly with his sister Ivy above her surgical appliance shop in Handbury Street, Whitechapel."

"No, pray be good enough to enlighten me, Inspector, I have not yet had a chance to consult the broadsheets. Help yourself to a Bradleys from the tin," said I.

"Queer, very queer indeed. I wonder, gentlemen, if you might care to accompany me back to Handbury Street; I just don't know what to make of it. We can take the underground."

Holmes crossed his long, lanky legs and frowned. "All this vague talk of a murder, Lestrade, has quite whetted my appetite to solve the matter. You and your colleagues at the Yard, I presume, are at a loss."

"Motiveless, utterly motiveless. The victim was well liked, known in local pubs, lived in Whitechapel all his life. Approachable, no disputes, irate neighbours

– a kind, considerable individual by all accounts, always willing to help others. Ivy, his sister, is distraught; for the life of her, she cannot understand how someone broke into the outside water closet in the back garden. No doubt a psychopath, both cunning and acquainted with the area. She claims she heard nothing. Mr Ellis, just before his evening meal, dinner on the table, visited the outside lavatory and had been gone for fifteen minutes when Ivy decided, food going cold, enough was enough and went to investigate. She was of the opinion the cistern was not functioning, the chain stuck. Her brother delayed in trying to fix the workings to make it flush properly, a common enough occurrence. However, when Miss Ellis hurried outside to the water closet, she was in for a real shocker. 'Orrible murder, that's what I call it, Mr Holmes. 'Orrible."

My companion sprang from his armchair, disrobing from this purple dressing gown and hurrying into his bedroom. "The suspense is palpable, tantalising. Let us lose not an instant, Inspector, Miss Ellis has need of us. We must hasten to Whitechapel at once. The fog lies thick, engulfing the capital, the subterranean railway, the Metropolitan & District, the East London line remains our surest and quickest means of achieving the East End. My dear Watson, this chilly, damp weather, the prevalent pea-souper indicates a warm scarf is requisite."

8

Whilst our steam locomotive advanced beneath London along the subsurface line, rattling through smoky, ill-ventilated tunnels, Lestrade remained uncharacteristically low in spirits, silent and thoughtful. However, I recall one topic which did get him out of his reverie was mention of that Kamens fire.

"Large fire was it?" enquired Holmes, puffing nonchalantly on his pipe.

"Eighteen pumps from all over London," the inspector sighed. "Incredible; warehouse and offices burnt to cinders. 'Empty at the time', according to managers," he mused, before once more withdrawing into himself, but I digress.

From Whitechapel underground we walked briskly through the fog, the half mile or so to Handbury Street consisting of a row of shops and a row of dingy terraced houses, a cabinet maker's gated yard at one end.

Entering the door to the modest surgical appliance shop with its dusty, somewhat jaded window display of various sizes of truss and wot-not, we were shown by a constable through to the back parlour where a chubby, homely matron I should judge of eight and fifty who, even with the burden of her brother's untimely death, scurrying about preparing cups and saucers, offered us tea, fussing over our every comfort. Police had instructed her brother's body should not be removed, which must have been doubly distressing, particularly, as I found out later, given the appalling nature of the injuries.

"My dear Miss Ellis," said Holmes, accepting his tea. "Forgive my intrusion at this sad time. My name is Sherlock Holmes and I am a consulting detective. This is my colleague Dr Watson. We are assisting Scotland Yard in the investigation and I promise I shall do everything in my power to bring the murderer of your dear brother to face summary justice in the courts. For now, however, I wish to ascertain his means of employment when alive and gain a little understanding of his character. I shall not detain you long. Do you smoke? No, well I shall light a cigarette if I may."

Miss Ellis passed around a tin of biscuits. "Well, sir, I cannot understand why my brother, known round here to be of a gentle and kindly disposition, always putting himself out for others with not an enemy in the world, should have been so cruelly done away with. He always loved his work. Since the age of thirteen he had been apprenticed to a local meat processing firm and was a slaughterhouse man by trade."

"A shift worker dealing with livestock – pigs, sheep and cattle."

"Indeed, Mr Holmes," she replied, taking out her hanky. "He was promoted to abattoir supervisor and due to retire next year. Lor', I was so proud of him," she sobbed.

"Thank you, Miss Ellis, that will suffice for now," my colleague voiced, somewhat abruptly, the woman in floods of tears being comforted by the attending constable. "Inspector, if we might view the ..."

"Of course, Mr Holmes, follow me," said Lestrade, a tad reprovingly, although by now well acquainted with my friend's want of tact. We were led into the back garden and along a short, paved path to where was situated in front of a hedge a shabby, shingle-roofed water closet roughly constructed of planks covered in moss, a loose- fitting door hanging off its hinges, wide open. What lay inside, slumped back on the lavatory seat, beggared belief.

"By Jove, what have we here?" exclaimed my esteemed colleague, assessing the state of the body with a practised eye. "Similarities, certainly," he said in a detached way. "What does the police surgeon make of it? More than one attacker involved, Lestrade?"

"The medical officer is not sure, Mr Holmes, and has yet to make an autopsy."

"Of course, so much cut and thrust of sharp blades. Watson, old fellow, I should value your opinion."

"Well, Holmes," said I, stooping over to gain a better diagnosis. "The appalling injuries are entirely consistent with a knife attack. Multiple lesions, the body eviscerated and, in the style, say, mimicking Jack the Ripper, the intestines slung over one shoulder. Liver and kidneys removed, put on display, the heart absent. The face utterly flayed and destroyed. What can be plainer? One is reminded of the crime photograph of Mary Kelly taken at Millers Court after her body was discovered. Could this be the work of Jack the Ripper? Is this, after a delay of so many years, yet another victim?" I concluded. The detective nodded in full agreement.

Holmes, well out of earshot of Inspector Lestrade, took me aside. "My dear Watson," said he, preparing me for a revelation, passing me a Bradleys from his silver cigarette case. "That gutted, mutilated thing in the water closet is Jack the Ripper. No, before you have me committed, hear me out." He kept his voice almost to a whisper. "Ellis is my perfect candidate. Have I not always said the Ripper was an ordinary person, an East Ender, well-liked by the community, living all his life in Whitechapel? A meat worker who fantasised about doing the same to women that he did daily in the abattoir to livestock."

"But Holmes, really ..."

"Listen, old chap, I've told you so many times, I believed he lived quietly with his mother or sister, visiting pubs, occasionally consorting with prostitutes who knew him as a bit of a lark, a soft touch for money and absolutely harmless."

"Granted, but how do you explain this vile murder? He couldn't have inflicted the injuries on himself, surely?"

"Watson, think back – to the warehouse – that infernal séance machine, how Major Churchward raised those five women, the victims of the Ripper."

"Yes, I recall that. Good heavens, you mean it was those plasmic forms, the transported spirits that are responsible – all five?"

"Exactly – an opportunity for sweet revenge. Certain of the girls must have known the identity of their murderer, been able to see his face just before they died. Ellis, mild-mannered, sweet- tempered Ellis, a slaughterhouse man with a lust which he could not quell nor control."

9

Travelling on the metropolitan railway to Baker Street through smoke-filled tunnels, our carriage insufferably hot, full of fumes from the gas lighting, my companion, completely at ease with his position, defended his decision to keep Inspector Lestrade entirely in the dark regarding his findings. For myself, I perfectly understood. Who on earth, of a sane mind and outlook, would credit vengeful spirit beings with cutting a man up in a water closet?

"So, the explosion and consequent fire at Kamens may not have obliterated this psychic process of regeneration as we hoped," said I, puffing on a cigarette. "The girls were able to transmute to Whitechapel and cause havoc," I pointed out.

"That appears to be the case, my dear Watson. We must remain on our guard in future. The spirits certainly don't need to travel by public transport, although the black box generator, as we know, was destroyed outright and it will take a considerable time to re-invent another such contraption. One supposes these fleshed out entities must have survived the intense heat that night in Horditch."

"Been unaffected."

"Quite. Poor Lestrade, I fear he will never ever be able to solve the Handbury Street murder, but I'm certain he will raise his game and provide us considerable breakfast time amusement speculating in the newspapers, offering all sorts of dud theories." I laughed heartily. "Ah, Holmes, Baker Street, we have arrived." I was about to get up – my companion paused.

"You know, I think we should proceed to Piccadilly Circus. I quite fancy a spanking good lunch at the Criterion, else mayhap beef at Simpsons – are you game, Watson?"

"Certainly," I answered, full of unmitigated admiration for my dear friend.

———

A fortnight later, upon a morning in which the fog persisted, ensconced in our front sitting room, Holmes, wearing his shabby, purple dressing gown, continually paced up and down before the fireplace, his head bowed, his hawk-like features presenting a determined, restless need for action. Slouching in my armchair, I, on the other hand, was perfectly content to be a lounger doing absolutely nothing that morning, save browse the sports pages. However, I knew what was needling him.

"The Hopkins issue will not simply go away, Holmes," said I, putting down my crumpled newspaper. "After all, you're being paid a substantial fee by the Psychic Society here in London to clear the matter up. Sir Oliver Lodge shall be expecting great things of you. We are established at least Dr Booth and Mr Cushing stole that Cromwellian boot for nefarious purposes."

My companion chose his long cherry-wood pipe from the rack on the mantelpiece, seizing the Persian slipper besides. "You do not have to remind me of my obligations, Watson," he replied, a certain amount of irritation evident in his voice. "That confounded boot snatched so audaciously is obviously associated with the modified séance we attended at the factory. What did old Churchward have to say? 'We shall raise Matthew Hopkins at half eight' or some such, therefore we deduce the boot is a psychic aid, a material link to the Witchfinder General and of tremendous importance to proceedings. That is why Cushing and Booth took such pains to steal it from Wigan Museum, one of them even dressing up as a woman, you recall."

I nodded, lighting a cigarette. "Of undoubted concern," I suggested, "is the fact that our deliberately started fire may not have been as effective as we wished."

"I realise that, but at least the black box generator was totally destroyed. Of that I'm certain; that'll set them back."

"The question is – did the fire take hold before or after Hopkins' transmigration – was he already 'fleshed out', in spiritual jargon, when the thing went bang, or did the pandemonium that ensued abort any attempt to bring the Witchfinder General back from the afterlife to reappear? Was there a delayed reaction, I wonder?"

Striking a vesta, my colleague lit his pipe, and leaning against the mantelshelf thought for a bit. "Well, Hopkins was due next, before the proposed coffee break at nine. How many of those lobotomised inmates of Hob Lane Infirmary connected to the electricity machine by cables were actually left alive by then is debatable, the tops of their heads plugged into the table, sapped of all their life force for the greater good. Most were dead, I suspect. I mean, on the face of it, the whole bally materialisation procedure is just too ruthless and dastardly for words. Even Sir Oliver Lodge should be seriously confounded that six old men were sacrificed and killed in order the spirits could regenerate, and yet, Watson, we bore witness."

I agreed entirely. "For example, the Ripper victims, Mary Jane Kelly, Katherine Eddowes, Elizabeth Stride and so forth, materialising – three dimensional certainly. But I recall a peculiar shimmering quality. They're not as solid as us."

"Exactly, dear boy, but look what those ethereal ladies got up to at Handbury Street. They can conceivably transmute and have no need of travelling by cab or horse bus from one place to another."

Puffing on his pipe, Holmes stared gloomily out of the bay window with nothing much in prospect save the infernal fog, now in its fourth week. "Ellis cut to ribbons, the Ripper no more," he mused.

"I can't get over those wily factory managers," said I, changing tack slightly, "in Major Churchward's pay, no doubt. Had the audacity to comment on the newspapers that the offices and warehouse damaged in the blaze were fully insured and empty at the time."

"Well, Churchward's the main shareholder, practically owns the place. He inherited the rubber works shares from his grandfather apparently. Look old fellow, the major, apart from his manufacturing interests, is a top psychic celebrity, possessed of clairvoyant powers, a medium widely in demand who earns a phenomenal amount of money from those circus style séance tours round Britain. He has immense monetary resources at his disposal. We know he is pally with the Fleet Street press barons. As yet, I am unable to pin him down. Obviously, by his association with Cawdaw, Troughton and Lambart, he has criminal leanings. Unsavoury representatives of the Horditch wheelchair gang were, after all, present at the séance. Have no fear, Watson, I shall undoubtedly get to the crux of the matter. But to think most people commonly associate séances with alphabet cards, bells, table rapping and the planchette. This advanced spirit communication is much more innovative and dynamic. One is aware we are treading on dangerous new ground."

"And what of poor old Toddy?" said I, wistfully. "Thanks to bedridden Mr Price, at least we were able to make some headway. If only we could have rescued him from that awful workhouse infirmary, could have done something, Holmes. Why don't you recount our fearful experience at Hob Lane to Inspector Lestrade, get the authorities to close the place down, Dr Booth struck off?"

"My dear fellow, I hardly think a poorhouse inmate will inspire much interest from the police. Corrupt goings on or otherwise, Toddy Price and the others will be buried under substantial quick lime in an unmarked pit by now. That, else incinerated in the warehouse fire. We are talking down-and-outs, remember – the dregs of society."

"We're talking human beings," I retorted, once more disappearing behind the outspread pages of my Daily Telegraph, disappointed, it must be said, at how both myself and Holmes let Mr Price down, acted so ineffectively at the time.

Relighting his pipe, my colleague chose to make some experiment with his chemistry set. At about noon, Mrs Hudson, bringing up our lunch of tender steak and baked potatoes and a pot of tea, passed

Holmes a recently arrived telegram delivered by the post boy. He perused the contents but briefly before expounding joyously: "Watson, pack at once. This is from the chief constable of Suffolk, no less. My consulting practice receives an unexpected boon, a manor house murder of Lady Pippa Baines-Clarke of Saxmundham, a country village on the Framlingham branch. An Inspector Tristram Irons based at Ipswich requests my assistance in solving the case. While journeying to Suffolk gives me the chance to refresh my memory regarding the Civil War period of Oliver Cromwell. By consulting Woods' three volume work, The History of England, one may be able to discern more of Hopkins' role. Ah, my dear Watson, could you fetch down my Burkes Peerage and Bradshaw's."

10

Bidding our landlady, Mrs Hudson, adieu, we bundled into a cab travelling much of the way to Kings Cross at a snail's pace due to fog hampering visibility; horse traffic for much of the way, congested and slow across London, being guided by flaming oil cans and torches at junctions and on street corners. We purchased a bundle of newspapers and were glad to find we had a first-class smoker to ourselves. Of course, being autumn, there were no tiresome summer tourists heading to Yarmouth and Lowestoft, and so forth. From Ipswich, a port and the capital of the county of Suffolk, we eventually attained the Framlingham branch where a short train travelled through Marlesford and Parham forward to Snape and Saxmundham, the line meandering coastwards to Leiston and the little watering place of Aldeburgh with its shingle beach.

My companion, lounging in the far corner, took out his sealskin pouch and began to fill his old briar pipe with shag tobacco. Confident and full of beans was how I preferred to see my friend, not beset by black moods or pondering use of the cocaine syringe.

Whilst the compartment filled with acrid tobacco fumes, I confess I was excited at the prospect of once again seeing my colleague focus his clever mind on a case, a manor house murder by the sound of it. Few details were available, although the detective Tristram Irons should never have requested my colleague's services unless there was some baffling difficulty the police were encountering, an impasse in which the official Suffolk force was found wanting.

"Suffolk," Holmes expounded as the train rattled along, indicating to the heavy calf- bound tome he had been reading, one of three history books piled beside him upon the cloth- covered seat. "One, of course, recalls the famous letter written by Oliver Cromwell defending an 'Anabaptist', and extreme Puritan, from censure by Major General Crawford. Then only a captain, of course, Cromwell was about to rapidly rise through the Roundhead army ranks – from small beginnings ...! He was alone responsible for creating the favoured post of Witchfinder General and appointing Matthew Hopkins."

"The great protector must have envisaged a real threat from witchcraft," said I. "What confounded twaddle."

"I suppose he did, Watson; thus Matthew Hopkins, more and more desirous of advancement and political clout, became totally ruthless, presenting trumped-up charges, falsifying evidence, ducking women at the drop of a hat – goading folk into testifying. Bushwick Manor, where we are headed, I read in my copy of Woods' History of England Volume III, during the seventeenth century was home to a member of the Roundhead old guard, Colonel Sir John Baines- Clarke of the new model army. Lady Pippa's late husband, Ronald, the M.P., would, of course, be related from a long line of military forbears."

"Well, you're certainly up on your history, old chap," said I, lighting my own pipe.

"Ah, the tea trolley appears. I think I shall sample one of that lady's most excellent buttered ham rolls," said he.

At Saxmundham, a quaintly picturesque station, we were met in the ticket hall by boyish Inspector Tristram Irons, a strapping young fellow wearing casual country tweeds, brandishing a stout ash stick, possessed of a healthy, ruddy, beetroot complexion and, I observed, sporting dundreary whiskers, then very much out of fashion since the sixties. His hair was well lubricated with bay rum. With his immense ham thighs, broad shoulders, stout chest and pudgy, pugilistic nose, I took him to be a sports enthusiast, a rugger scrum-half, perhaps. Whatever, he appeared unusually young to have achieved the grade of inspector, proving most convivial company, intelligent besides.

"Well, Mr Holmes, I am delighted to make your acquaintance, and you also Dr Watson. Your reputation as a consulting detective who gets results is reason enough to bring you up here from London, although the weather in Suffolk appears somewhat cold and overcast."

"But at least no pea-soupers, young man," I laughed as we placed our luggage in the rear of the waggonette.

"A wholly, most unedifying murder," said Holmes, climbing up onto the box seat. "According to my Burke's Peerage, Lady Baines-Clarke is the widow of the late M.P. and government minister, Sir Ronald, who was a brigadier in the army. I am anxious to view for myself the scene. By the by, is there a bed and board you could recommend, Irons?"

"I have booked you, gentlemen, rooms at The Swan. Mrs Lockwood will look after you, serve your meals; she is a first-rate proprietor and cook. The inn is but a short distance from the manor."

"Excellent, then let us lose no time. The body of Lady Baines-Clarke has not, I trust, been disturbed, Inspector. I hate to cast aspersions, to imply incompetence, else clumsiness, on the part of Suffolk constabulary, yet from bitter past experience, one simply dreads vital evidence being destroyed."

"Most certainly not, sir, and no offence taken. A police surgeon briefly examined the body, but left things straight and tidy. I can vouch for that."

We eventually, having stopped off at The Swan to unload our carpet bags, trotted through the little village with its market cross and mid-sixteenth century church, and arrived at Bushwick Manor.

Accompanied by a Mrs Hooper, the head housekeeper, our party was led by a constable away from the handsome Palladian mansion round past the topiary hedges to a wintry and barren orchard. The sight that greeted us was terribly unsettling, for an elderly woman hung strangled some four feet off the ground, her neck forced between the forked branches of a gnarled old fruit tree, a hazel broomstick of twigs, practical and ideal for sweeping leaves from path and lawn at this time of year, draped from her neck, the haft tied by green garden twine; beneath her slightly swaying slippers, amongst the tufty grass, a cheap, plain, wood crucifix, a flayed domestic cat, both these bordered by neatly spaced pebbles laid out in a ritualistic, if childish, fashion, a note pinned to the strangled woman's breast, written in atrocious scrawl, stated:

I am of a sin-disquieted soul

"The inference is plain," remarked my colleague caustically, unable to conceal his slight disappointment. "Our murderer gains full marks for effect; a strong hint, I think. I had expected better. However, Mrs Hooper, do you smoke? No? Allow me to pass round my cigarette case. Help yourself, Irons."

The chill, wintry weather and rapidly fading light inclined me towards a good dinner and bottle of Chablis back at The Swan.

My friend persisted: "Pray, can you identify any of the accoutrements – the remains, the carcass of the skinned cat, for example, Mrs Hooper?"

I can, sir, the cat's name is "Tolpuddle.Black."

"Most assuredly, Mr Holmes. It was my mistress' favourite. He was a beautifully tempered and affectionate animal and followed her about everywhere; he curled up on her bed at night."

"The plain, cheap, wooden crucifix?"

"I recall was kept in a drawer in the kitchen dresser along with a muddle of odds and ends."

"We now require to return to the main house where I shall interview members of staff. Mrs Hooper, please go on ahead and prepare the way; the kitchen would suit admirably, Inspector Irons. Her Ladyship's body may be decently removed."

The interview primarily concerned Mr Grobb the head butler, Miss Walton the cook, Florrie Benson and Annie Husker, under-maids, Miss Evline and Mr Seymour the gardener.

The gardener rose from his chair and agreed the hazel broom was indeed missing from its usual hook in the shed round by the glasshouses. Miss Evline, just by her facial expression, conveyed genuine grief and puzzlement, and disgust at the fate of Lady Baines-Clarke's favourite pet. Mr Grobb's movements could all be accounted for; similarly, pretty, demure Miss Walton with her sweet, natural tone. Likewise, Florrie Benson and Annie Husker who, typical of the younger generation, despite the gravitas of their employer's death in the orchard, seemed to find amusement from Holmes' stiff and rather formal, owl-like stance, barely able to contain their giggles. My colleague lit a cigarette and passed me his silver case.

"You girls travelled to London, you say, Miss Benson, to see a West End play, a matinee performance at the Wimborne Theatre in Drury Lane of Gregory's Ghost starring Charles Lemon. You, Miss Benson and Miss Husker, possess, I perceive, superlative taste, for Dr Watson and myself attended a first night performance and enjoyed it immensely. Charles and his impresario business partner, Langton Lovell, run the theatre and are dear friends of ours. I think that is all for now. You may attend to your household duties."

Thank goodness the long, galling interview period came to a close and everybody was able to disperse. Her Ladyship's sister, Ferne, from Long Melford, was due to take over the running of Bushwick Manor, coming to live there so one was aware of an immense sense of relief amongst the staff, who should at least, despite the crisis, be able to retain their posts.

"Not much to go on is there?" said I in a vague way, replacing my cap and scarf as we stepped outside into the cold. My friend kept wise council.

"I think exercise is requisite," said he, pursing his lips, "most beneficial. We shall cycle to The Swan and take in the good, Suffolk air, Watson."

Thus, Holmes badgered the old gardener, Mr Seymour, into lending us a pair of machines. He returned shortly with two gleaming Townsend Tourers, sulphur lamps lit and ready.

Bidding the inspector good evening and suggesting we meet early at half past six at The Swan for a conference, promising he was pursuing certain lines of enquiry, Holmes tore on ahead, cycling along the main street like fury, his red rear light reflecting dimly in the darkness. I struggled to keep up with him. Pedalling like mad, I eventually drew into the kerb and dismounted, but Holmes kept on riding.

The Swan, a thatched roofed, half-timbered country hotel-cum-public house, looked most inviting with lamplight glowing from the windows. "Go in and order dinner, old chap," he called back. "I'm absolutely famished. I shall be back presently. Our luggage we dropped off earlier and our rooms should be ready. I won't be more than ten minutes."

Later, seated in the cosy oak-panelled snug, we consumed the most appetising of meals. "Your culinary skills are unsurpassed, the lamb cutlets quite delicious. Forgive my prying, Mrs Lockwood, but to your knowledge was Lady Clarke likely to be a practising witch, or a modern day equivalent, obviously not the hag-ridden, warty variety so beloved of children's fairy tales. For argument's sake, I could not help observing the extensive medicinal herb garden, the ring of trees furthermost across the grounds, so redolent of a magical circle. Was the mistress of Bushwick Manor a member of a coven? Are you yourself, perhaps, a witch, Mrs Lockwood?"

"Me, a witch? I believe not, Mr Holmes, and I can hardly be expected to answer for Her Ladyship," our charming hostess replied pleasantly, passing us bowls of rhubarb crumble and custard. "But I shall not be backward here," said she in a hushed voice. "It is widely rumoured that Saxmundham..."

"... is historically associated with witchcraft. Yes, I catch your drift."

Mrs Lockwood nodded. "I shall be frank, Mr Holmes; Pippa, a sprightly sixty-year-old, was prone to wander naked on nights of the full moon in the grounds of the manor. She danced free and uninhibited in the glade of trees you mention with others. Her Ladyship would have referred to this as 'moon-bathing', expressing the inner self. Herbs were a passion of hers. Up at the manor, she did produce excellent soaps from vegetable oil, not whale fat, and lip balm and sundry 'pep me up' tonics. I can vouch for the quality and care which went into the products – but she was never seen flying on a broomstick, nor consorting with Old Nick, or threatening to turn that ugly, morose butler of hers, Mr Grobb, into a toad. How wonderfully exhilarating if she could."

"Alas, to those of a superstitious turn given to spitefulness and gossip, afraid of free expression, they, Mrs Lockwood, should ascribe her behaviour as being in league with the devil and that black cat of hers as evilly disposed."

The next morning, as agreed, Inspector Tristram Irons arrived early at The Swan, chirpy as a lark and eager to analyse Holmes' deductions, probe his findings. Taking his place in the hotel lounge, the young detective was fussed over by Mrs Lockwood and partook of a plate of kippers which he devoured with relish.

Lighting his after-breakfast pipe, blowing out a good deal of smoke, my companion proceeded to detail certain discrepancies. "They were not telling the truth. Florrie Benson and Annie Husker, on the twenty-third, travelled on to Ipswich, not down to London to see a play. I enquired at the station last night. The ticket clerk recalls seeing the girls, whom he is familiar with. Also, he remembers the fares and destination; London was not, and never had been, on their agenda."

"Why," said I, "this is a serious development, Holmes. When Lady Clarke was murdered, she was presented rather dubiously as a suicide, which of course failed to fool the Suffolk police, nor us. But two persons involved – well, well."

"And, of course, in no possible way was Her Ladyship strangulated, killed in the manner presented. Lady Clarke's clothes were just too neatly arranged, impeccably ironed, clean and well creased. The ground over the past few days should surely have been damp and muddy, especially at night, yet her slippers were spotless. Her face held no expression of violent suffocation. Not one sign of struggle, scratches, bloody fingernails, fighting for one's life as surely a determined woman of her class should exhibit in the face of provocation."

"Poisoned earlier, you infer, Mr Holmes? By Harry, that makes sound sense," admitted the detective, wiping his chin with a napkin. "Then carried outside to the orchard by the two under- maids, both well strong enough, making her out to be a suicide."

"Strychnine – in her night-time hot chocolate. There is nothing new under the sun, Inspector. Oh, I shouldn't be surprised if the autopsy shall reveal a probable quantity of alkali in her system. You see, Irons, Lady Clarke was most likely poisoned when they – that is Benson and Husker – helped her undress for bed, which, I was informed by Mrs Hooper, was among their duties."

"But why?" I asked, tamping down strands of my favourite Arcadia mixture into the bowl of my pipe. "Why was she done away with?"

"That is not too difficult too determine, Watson," said Holmes, lazily reaching his long arm into a waste bin near his chair. He retrieved a somewhat tea-slopped, well-stained copy of the Suffolk Herald that I had noticed he perused earlier, passing time before Mrs Lockwood served breakfast – an old, outdated edition. "This is for the twenty-first of the month. As Watson can verify, Inspector, as is my habit, I invariably study the local flavour of the newsworthy items, paying special regard to the personal columns and advertisements. Here, you notice, we see plainly advertised for the evening of the twenty-third at Ipswich town hall an item of considerable merit. So, what do you make of it, my dear Watson?"

IPSWICH TOWN HALL
THE HOPKINITES

A society dedicated to the celebration of the interesting life of M Hopkins the mediaeval philanthropist, friend to the poor and needy, who, through her charitable works, introduced the first alms houses and hospitals into Suffolk and Norfolk. Mary Hopkins is remembered – tonight 7:30pm. Coffee and tea provided.

I frankly confess my brow contracted into a positive frown.

"Woods' History of England, Volume One, referring to mediaeval Suffolk, makes no mention of a Mary Hopkins," my colleague informed us, puffing on his short pipe.

"Good gracious, Holmes," I ejaculated. "What is this all about? The surname, surely, has sinister connotations as far as we are concerned?"

"I shall elaborate, if I may. I have a strong intuition regarding the real agenda of the so-called Hopkinites. It will soon become abundantly clear, Inspector, that Lady Baines-Clarke was murdered because, by marriage to the M.P. Ronald, she became related to a long line of military forbears, among them, during the period of the Civil War, a high-ranking officer in the new model army; a Roundhead by the name of Sir John Baines- Clarke, and it was he I believe to be chief among conspirators who planned and took it upon themselves to assassinate, at Cromwell's Ditch in Wigan where the Witchfinder General was attending a trial at the time, a man then becoming notorious throughout the land for his relentless pursuit of witches and mounting tally of market square hangings. 'M' Hopkins refers to Matthew, not Mary."

Without further ado, we hurried up the street to Bushwick Manor. Upon entering the tradesmen's entrance round by the kitchen door, Holmes lost no time in hustling the two under-maids into the kitchen for questioning. He kept his attitude always cheerful and effete – appearing very friendly towards the girls.

"My dear young ladies," Holmes trilled gaily. "Could you spare a minute to tell us what you thought of Gregory's Ghost? I personally found the play an absolute scream from first to last. The funniest bit was when Saunders, the raving butler, collided with the apparition. That's it, do sit down."

"Oh yes, that was very funny. Yes, I agree, don't you, Annie?"

"What? Oh yes, very funny," the other answered in a bored, disinterested way, yawning hugely. "Watson, do you ever actually recall a butler colliding on stage with the ghost?"

"Never," said I, filling my pipe, "because it didn't happen."

"You're not telling us the truth, ladies," said Inspector Irons, keeping commendably calm and grinning.

"Now that we have established you did not attend Drury Lane on the twenty-third, might I ask what you were doing in Ipswich?"

"We were never in Ipswich," replied Benson, also yawning. "We went to London – ended up seeing the sights. What's that to do with you?"

"You lie. Both of you were in Ipswich to attend a meeting of 'the Hopkinites' at the town hall. You, Benson, and you too, Husker, I charge as being chosen emissaries of a society you have belonged to for some time. Your characters are, I perceive, both surly and cunning, you are of a slatternly type, easily influenced, I suspect susceptible to the charms of men. Was it Major Churchward, or a Mr Cushing who first approached you, informing you that the spirit of Matthew Hopkins would soon be back on earth and that the Witchfinder had indicated by means of a planchette he wanted Lady Baines-Clarke eradicated, his reason, an old score to settle?"

"She was a witch-whore," Annie Husker screamed. "We witnessed her and the others cavorting under the moon in unholy alliance with the old goat Satan hisself, both naked and ecstatic. I saw it all."

"We reported her as such," cried the other, staring at us wildly, her face spread in panic. "She was a witch-whore, gone over to the devil. All witches shall perish and those that side with them."

Allowing Benson her plainly ridiculous rant, Irons had heard enough.

"I am arresting you for the murder of Lady Baines-Clarke," said the detective, solemnly taking no nonsense and expertly applying one set of cuffs, I the other, quickly securing the domestics' wrists.

"I fear you are indoctrinated, your endeavours misguided," said my colleague coldly. "You callously poisoned your mistress when you were about to help her undress before bed, her drinking chocolate tainted, thereafter looking out for one another. You deliberately carried her out into the garden and, in an attempt to hoodwink the police, arranged her like a suicide, presenting Her Ladyship as a woman deeply racked by guilt and despair. None of us were fooled. By the by, the second coming of your master, Hopkins, is indefinitely delayed due to a factory fire. And now, Watson, I believe we have a train to catch. The Pullman service on the 2:25 from Ipswich to London is, I hear, a first-rate dining facility. Let us lose no time in catching the connection."

———

A week since the Hopkinite affair at Saxmundham found me a committed idler with time on my hands. Slumped in my armchair, a novel concerning naval battles perched on the arm, whilst the clock chimed the half hour and coal spat, crackling in the grate behind the brass fireguard, I pondered once more the unfolded tobacco pouch on my lap, empty of 'Ships', my preferred mixture.

Rousing myself sufficiently, I went over and nosed into our threadbare Persian slipper, empty again. Choosing not to sample the stale dottles pertaining to Holmes' many smokes of the day before piled on the corner of the mantelshelf, I decided it timely to visit Bradley's the tobacconist, taking the horse-bus to Oxford Street.

"Yes, Watson," murmured my colleague, coiled up in his fireside chair, draped in his shabby dressing gown holed by chemical burns, his hair ruffled and unkempt. "Five ounce bag of shag, four tins of 'ready-mades'," said he. "Got that?"

Barely glancing up from his newspaper, his wan, pinched features were lost in concentration. I recall after such a manic, eventful November, a very busy month, we, on the whole, were inclined to be lethargic, loath to venture far from our front sitting room, the perpetual pea-soupers partly to blame, but also a genuine need for recuperation.

This frosty morning, however, at the beginning of December, sunny, bright and crisp, a hot potato and chestnut vendor doing a brisk trade up by the bookshop, I confess I felt perked up, renewed vigour. Determined to get out and stretch my legs, I was about to go upstairs and dress. "Poor old Toddy," I said under my breath, heading for the landing. "Mr Price, if only we'd acted sooner, cared a weeny bit more."

"Nonsense!" remarked Holmes irritably, crossing his long, lanky legs, shaking out the pages of The Telegraph. "I am sympathetic, like you, appalled at his eventual fate, but what was one to do? That infirmary was dratted secure, the place an institutionalised poorhouse."

"Granted," said I, "but for argument's sake, if Toddy had been a privileged member of society – a banker, a chairman of some concern – would we have acted differently, come up more to the mark?"

"Possibly, Watson, possibly. Now, dear boy, put old Toddy out of your mind, and for heaven's sake, concentrate on Bradleys. My dottles shall serve for now, of course."

Rather miffed, I was about to quit the room when the noise of a hansom clattering to a halt outside our doorstep alerted our attention. I paused, tying my dressing gown together. One could hear from downstairs a firm rap at the door knocker, a man's clipped, brusque enquiry, heavy footfalls upon the stair.

"Mycroft!" cried my companion exultantly, slinging aside his paper, darting to the mantelshelf collecting dottles and stuffing his long pipe. "His extreme bodily weight is apparent, wheezing as he steps onto the landing. Well, I say, no harm in a little exercise. You know, my brother rarely ventures Marylebone way; a visit to our digs can only mean he has a matter of a most serious nature to discuss.

Government mole, missing crown documents, perhaps."

"Sherlock!" My colleague's elder, heavily obese brother burst into our rooms, immaculately turned out in opera cloak, frock coat and spats. He removed his satin topper, slinging this, together with his gold-handled cane, upon the sofa, warming his considerable bulk in front of the fireplace before himself, that is the immense weight of the man, went crashing into the sofa's depths and cushioning. "Anthony, the silly, silly boy," he gasped, shaking his mane of white hair, his red face adorned by those unrivalled, grizzled, Piccadilly whiskers of his. He placed a gold monocle to his left eye.

"My dear Mycroft," said my colleague amiably. "You have the advantage of me. I perceive by your folded copy of The Times you have ringed in red ink an item of very minor interest concerning a carriage accident in Monroe Street. Anthony? Anthony who?"

"Blasted fool is what Anthony Sterling is. You know, Sherlock, the bespoke milliner in Bond Street. Her Majesty simply adores his hats, ladies in high society vie for his creations, but now there's dark times ahead. He and his partner, Johnny Bernard, are members of the Diogenes – ahem, you comprehend my earlier emphasis upon the word 'partner', I trust."

My colleague, puffing on his long pipe, nodded. "They share a life together, both business and social. But what's all this got to do with an inconsequential carriage accident? Of course, regrettably there was a fatality."

"Inconsequential? Bah, if only that were the case. Yes, I will have a cup of Mrs Hudson's Brazilian ground coffee, thank you, Watson." Holmes' portly elder brother paused to accept a cup and saucer. "Carriage stopped in the street," he expounded, smacking his lips, sampling the coffee. "Damn blackmailer. If only Anthony and Johnny were more discreet, wining and dining at the basement club 'The Wages of Sin'. Bound to have repercussions."

"The short piece you ringed informs the reader of a city carriage accident. Someone in an invalid chair crossing the road struck down. Nothing to do with that notorious Soho club."

"That's the rub, Sherlock. You see, Anthony's groom, Mr Crumm, a most reliable and faithful servant, insists, swears, in fact, that this old disabled man deliberately chucked himself and his wheeled chair under the trotting horses. I mean, that's just insane. The poor, poor fellow." Mycroft dabbed his leonine forehead with a handkerchief.

"Oh, the disabled chap run down," said I. "As a doctor, when a married man with a practice in Paddington, I attended many such incidences. Alas, if not severely maimed, the victim rarely survives. Terrible limb and head fractures result. Saddest are the street urchins, the children caught up and killed during the weeks of fog."

"What?" replied Mycroft. "No, I refer to Anthony Sterling, Dr Watson. Poor fella's a sensitive type, artistic. He felt the embarrassment of the situation so keenly. Traffic got held up for ages. Queues of horse buses full of irate passengers wanting to get on; mortuary ambulance ages to arrive. But, far worse, well, confound it all, this other chappie, most likely an accomplice, wearing a flat cap, also in a wheeled chair, had the brazen impudence, the audacity to start shouting abuse from the pavement at the Queen's personal milliner. But you see, there was cunning behind this florid rant, for the common fellow, after rousing bad feeling, spitting at Anthony, passes him an envelope into the carriage before withdrawing, vanishing into the crowd."

"Presumably you have the note? Pass it over – allow me to peruse it briefly."

I hereto provide the reader with an accurate facsimile:

Dear Johnny and Anthony,

Whilst in Soho the other night, I acquired a set of glass negative plates. Both of you a wee bit tipsy, having such a jolly time, dancing at the 'Wages of Sin' club with those young corporals from the army barracks. What fun, what hilarity when the police and press agencies receive

'photograph complimentaries'.

Not a word to anyone, mind. For now 2,000 guineas to be paid in cash. Leytonstone cemetery, Mary Kelly's plot, 6pm tonight or else...

Yours Awfully

Frightfully Nicely

Holmes, caring not a jot, threw the note into the crackling flames of the fire. Replacing his pipe on the rack he said, ebulliently, "You are in considerable luck, dear brother, for Dr Watson and I are already acquainted with this 'Mr Anon'. I believe our correspondent to be Ralphy Brown, an ex-Baker Street Irregular turned 'bad penny', a disgrace that I shall have to live with. Extortion, it appears, is his speciality. He is actively involved with the notorious Horditch wheelchair gang at a very high level. Presumably your chum, Anthony Sterling, kept his appointment with the blackmailer at Leytonstone. Six o'clock, wasn't it?"

"No damn choice, Sherlock. Gripped by fear at the unwanted publicity, the untold ruination that should come his way if he failed to comply. Travelled to Essex by train in an utter state of nerves. His hands were shaking when he handed over the canvas bag containing the loot. Legged it straight back to the Diogenes and wisely, over a dinner of first-rate oysters and foie gras, explained to me his dire predicament."

Whilst his erstwhile brother had been replying, my companion, meanwhile, concerned himself, sat at his desk, sorting through his bottles of chemicals, adding crystals to various solutions, shaking test tubes vigorously before pouring a quantity into a pair of separate glass beakers.

"Was the person he met at the graveside able bodied, or disabled?"

"Shifty cad wearing a low brimmed hat and thick scarf covering their features. Long, full-length overcoat."

"My dear Mycroft," said my colleague, striking a vesta to relight his cherry-wood pipe. "You may assure Anthony Sterling I shall look into the matter. I should very much like to become reacquainted with Ralph Brown whom Watson and I spoke briefly with at The Earl of Berkeley public house not so long ago."

"One might consider him an up-and-coming East London working-class version of Augustus Milverton," I proffered. My colleague visibly tensed and gave me a scathing glance which cut me to the quick.

"The late Augustus Milverton of Hampstead was in a class of his own, Watson. One of the richest, most successful blackmailers London has ever seen. Mycroft, might I press you for the address of the mortuary the disabled fellow's body was taken to for autopsy after the road accident?"

"London Authority. That would be Metropolitan Ward, 48 Dewer Street, W1. You know, the small church-like edifice attached to the police station."

Hailing a hansom along Baker Street, we bid farewell to Mycroft who was due to attend a meeting at Admiralty House with a naval attaché, promising to keep him updated on developments. Rattling across the capital, we attained the designated mortuary for the W1 district at midday. Upon entering the building, we were greeted by Dr Pardoe, the police surgeon known to us from previous cases, a first-rate pathologist.

"Ah, Mr Holmes, and you also Dr Watson. Delighted, I'm sure. What brings you out here on such a freezing day to our little mortuary? I'm afraid at present no baffling local murders – only two retained. A person who fell off a ladder, and upon this nearest trestle table we have a disabled chap. A pauper, undernourished, filthy dirty, brought in after being run over in Monroe Street. Chest awfully crushed, both legs snapped. Dr Watson, step this way."

We were promptly shown into the tiled mortuary. "Standard autopsy procedures performed on a body by myself and an assistant earlier this morning. Interestingly, a constable informed us, pedestrians, passers-by who witnessed the road accident along Monroe Street swear this disabled chap manoeuvred his wheeled chair straight out into the road, deliberately into the path of the oncoming carriage. Mad or what! The result we see lain out before us upon the nearest trestle table. Gather round; top of the head's had recent surgery."

Attired in his gauntlet gloves and apron, the police pathologist drew back the rubber sheet. Plucking a spatula from a trolley, the pathologist indicated to the scalp the electricity burns scorching the flesh where wired-up electrodes had been implanted either side of the man's head, Dr Booth's clever surgery, of course, easily recognisable. But as the sheet lowered further still, although the hair had grown back a bit, the face was that of our old acquaintance, our hero of the infirmary.

"Great Scott!" I exclaimed. "It's Toddy Price. What are we to make of this, Holmes?"

The police surgeon seemed unconcerned, his thoughts elsewhere. "A constable you know, gentlemen, informed me the carriage involved in the fatal collision was a chaise and pair belonging to Anthony Sterling, that high society milliner always in the papers. Does all the Queen's hats," said the surgeon.

"Yes, Sterling's of Bond Street," said my colleague tersely, leaning over to examine the electrodes carefully with his magnifying lens.

"Watson," commented the pathologist, "you seem perplexed. Surely, like me, both as a degree student at Barts and in the army, you've seen worse fractures than these."

"Oh, nothing to do with the trauma," I replied, pulling myself together. "I seem to recall this fellow's face." I left it at that, quickly recovering my composure.

"Mr Holmes, may I point out these wired electrodes?" requested the pathologist. "If I may elaborate, my own view is that this disabled chappie was, in life, an inmate, a patient of some specialist hospital for those with mental afflictions. Tooting Bec,

I'm told, has certain wards where they use helpful electricity shock therapy."

"Quite likely, implants for healthily applied voltage current, yes. I think your theory holds some merit," my colleague agreed with a quizzical smile, indicating we should leave for we had a train to catch.

"Mentally impaired, from a south London hospital, I expect," added Dr Pardoe, sounding very pleased with himself, guiding us through the door.

11

Situated upon the Woodford and Loughton branch, a line seven- and three-quarter miles long, skirting the borders of Epping Forest, Leytonstone is the next stop beyond Low Leyton station. Some readers, no doubt, are familiar with the little local church in which are deposited the remains of Strype, the noted antiquarian. The municipal cemetery lies but a short trudge from the station and, in modern times, like Brookwood Necropolis, a growing number of Londoners choose to be buried there.

One recalls Mary Kelly's public funeral in October 1888, funded by popular subscription, a good turnout, recorded in both national broadsheets and local dailies.

Her plot we discovered fairly easily traipsing about the rows of graves. It was presentable, tidy, a pewter urn or vase full of colourful blooms laid at the base of the headstone. Even in December, somebody cared enough to visit the cemetery on her behalf; most commendable.

However, I must report certain weird symbols scratched about defacing the granite, cabbalistic in design, at odds, somewhat, with the good Christian surroundings. I shivered, for it was growing colder, a chill wind blowing about this sepulchral region, the earlier sunshine replaced by lowering dark cloud.

Holmes flipped open his silver cigarette case, offering me a Bradleys which I gratefully accepted. "Regularly tended," he remarked. "Even at this time of year, mould sponged off the funerary masonry with soft soap, a pewter urn of fresh blooms. Mary Kelly has a stalwart admirer, far from forgotten, it seems."

"Relations."

"Possibly."

"Contrasting, somewhat, are those inscribed marks defacing the gravestone. They strike me as cabbalistic, magical symbols," said I, leaning forward to inspect more closely. "Some guardian hex nonsense, one supposes."

"Yet no one has thought to remove them. Most singular, they are fairly worn carvings, the precision use of a well-honed chisel, not the random work of an opportunist vandal."

Not caring if the grass was damp, Holmes spent some time checking and rechecking the surrounding shorn turf for footprints, using his trusty magnifying lens, as always, to great effect.

"You have discovered a useful print," said I, as my companion sprang up, unaware of his muddy knees.

"Indeed, I am clearer on certain movements and now, Watson, let us venture forth to the cemetery keeper's lodge near the entrance gates; we might glean certain useful data concerning Mary Kelly's ardent admirer."

Upon stepping under the porch, the architecture of the cemetery lodge aping the European Gothic style with steeply pitched roof, grimoire laden, spiky chimney pots, the gutter and leaded windows decorated by a profusion of carved stone dressings and gargoyles.

My friend briskly rang the bell-pull. Not long after, the keeper opened the front door. A genial, attentive individual, he was no doubt well used to visitors' enquiries and, puffing on his pug pipe, proved most helpful. "Good day," said my frock-coated, over six-feet-four tall, rake-thin companion, courteously removing his top hat. "So dreadfully sorry to bother you."

"Not at all. Mr Dalton at your service, gentlemen."

"Your waste bins are immaculate, the cleanest receptacles for litter I have ever seen. Rubbish is, I suppose, emptied regularly, even in winter."

"You are most kind, sir, one of the few to recognise the hard work of my ground staff. Yes, in winter, of course, we tend not to get such an accumulation of old worn floral tributes and tatty wreaths, flower husks and general litter. Bins are emptied less or'ften, not for the last fortnight or so."

"I wonder, keeper, could you tell me – do many gravetenders, that is friends and relatives, visit Leytonstone cemetery during autumn and winter? Me and Francis, here, are ever so impressed by Mary Kelly's tidy plot – so spick and span."

"Oh, that'd be Kay Vernon. Now, she is a regular. Even snow won't keep her away. Kay Vernon is most dedicated. For years, each week without fail, out here at Leytonstone in all weathers. Some, I suppose, might regard her slavish devotion as obsessive, respecting the memory of Mary Kelly. Mary Jane – Lord bless her departed soul, the fifth of the Ripper's victims that fateful October in 1888. Damn 'ees dark deeds. 'Ole Leather Apron' or 'Jacky the Terror' is his more correct title, by the way. I'se alus make a point of putting visitors right over that."

"Fascinating, Mr Dalton, you are something of an authority, I fancy. Is there a growing emergence of a Mary Kelly cult, I wonder?"

"Nothing would surprise me, gentlemen. Violent, newsworthy murders inevitably bring celebrity. Many come from all over London to pay their respects. In summer, mostly, of course, even Americans and the Chinese."

"But you are an authority."

"Mary Jane Kelly is buried here at Leytonstone, her grave is noteworthy, so I am naturally required to be informed."

"Do you, perchance, know much of Mrs Vernon? Her grave tending efforts are admirable. One is bound to say Mary Jane must mean an awful lot to her."

"Privacy is privacy, gentlemen," replied the keeper loftily. "My policy has always been never to enquire into people's backgrounds. Leytonstone cemetery, I pride myself, is a place of peace and repose. Folk come here to be with departed loved ones, and I am always respectful of this."

Bidding the keeper farewell, we trudged back the way we had come to Mary Kelly's plot. "Well, Holmes," I said, "we gleaned little useful data regarding this Kay Vernon."

My friend was about to answer when his attention was distracted. I watched as, like a hooded raptor, he hurried across the cemetery path to an iron litter bin. Stretching his long arm into its depths, furiously rummaging about, it was not long before he retrieved a scrunched-up piece of light tissue paper. I crossed over to join him. "Any joy with that bit of paper?" I asked, knowing so well by the expression upon his lean, hawk-like features he had discovered a crucial clue.

"This is our way forward. I have established already it was Mrs Vernon who herself acted as an intermediary for Ralph Brown. It was she who received the 2,000 guineas obtained by menaces. Her disguise, concealing though it was, the low hat and scarf and full length coat, failed to take into account a female's dainty size of footwear, the imprints of her high-heeled boots clear to see under the lens. I identified the recent prints of two persons over by the verge."

I took out my tin of cigarettes and offered him one. Lighting it, he continued: "But, returning to this flimsy sheet of tissue paper of the sort used when wrapping flowers, this litter bin is conveniently close to Mary Kelly's plot, so I'm thinking it was discarded by Mrs Vernon when she last spruced up the grave."

"By jingo, you're definitely onto something," I exclaimed, seizing my friend's arm. I concentrated upon his every word.

"Furthermore, my dear Watson – using this lens, it is not difficult to determine a faint watermark."

"A florist's," said I, "local to East London. Minerva Clements of Hob Lane, it says. Thus, it likely follows Mrs Vernon lives close by in the neighbourhood."

"Precisely."

12

From the surface railway, we ventured yet again below ground upon the smoky subterranean line tunnelled beneath East London, eventually pulling in at Hob Lane underground station. Ascending in the rickety lift, the gate drawn back, we found ourselves in the ticket hall opposite a wide view of the High Street.

"My dear Watson," said my friend, grabbing my arm, his lean, hawk-like features alive with curiosity. "How portentous – Clements the florist's only across the road, although it's late evening, still open for business. My, my, I find that rubber odour most stimulating to the nostrils."

"Promoting sinusitis," I remarked, aware of the tainted air. Walking at a brisk pace, we entered the premises cheerily disposed to the proprietor as the doorbell pinged.

"Good evening, sirs. I am Mrs Clements. How may I help?"

Aged, I should say, seven and sixty, wearing a green pinafore, her chubby face rosy cheeked, the lady smiled warmly. Presently, she was tucking tufts of moss into a wire frame, creating a Christmas wreath; beneath her bench, pails full of holly sprigs, ferns and evergreens. "We 'ave lovely hot-house lilies, hyacinth bulbs in pots. What's on? Wedding, bunch of flowers for yer sweetheart?" She approached us, wiping her glistening hands on a cloth.

"We are a trifle lost," my colleague explained. "Hoping to see dear Mrs Vernon. Number six, isn't it? Y'know, I wrote the number down on the back of a dratted cigarette card somewhere." My colleague fumbled uselessly in his pockets. This provoked in the kindly, hard-working shopkeeper a motherly response; an outpouring of sound sense followed.

"Just look at you – what you need, dear, is a proper address book. Never mind, Mrs Clements'll put you right. Dunno, mind, how she puts up with looking after a bloomin' lotta good-for-nothing, lazy scroungers. All them old men. Anyhow, twenty years ago, Kay, that is, Mrs Vernon, a goodly, pure-hearted widow, mind – was appointed by directors, guardians of the Poor Law Board, matron of the Hob Lane workhouse. She's in charge, along with the medical officer, Dr Booth, who is the master, a lovely, friendly gentleman; he always stops by for a chat when he's out walking his lurcher. The workhouse is just up the road, on your right. Got that?"

"You have been most kind, Mrs Clements. I will take a bunch of your most excellent ferns, if I may." My friend took out his wallet.

Whilst the florist plucked a selection of ferns from her bucket, wrapping them in tissue paper, Mrs Clements could not resist imparting an item of local gossip. "Now, gentlemen," she prattled on, "it so happens, last September they had a pantry-man, Sid Carter, who got sentenced to one month's imprisonment for stealing butter and margarine worth six shillings. Sacked, he were. Rate payers round 'ere demanded an enquiry."

"Talking of criminality, Mrs Clements, might I also broach the topic of the infamous wheelchair gang? I read of their exploits – a daring bank raid narrowly foiled."

"Ralphy Brown comes callin' end of every month. I pay 'im protection money. There, I've said enough. Goodnight, gentlemen."

Departing the florist's shop, we chose to remain in the area of the High Street, a winter's evening in the

East End, the tenements, rough lodging houses and back-to-backs – pubs like The Earl of Berkeley, the gin palace further up, the nearby gasworks and Kamens factory over by the sidings engulfed in darkness. A host of dingy, cobbled streets and alleys hemmed in by derelict housing feebly illumined by rows of wrought-iron gas lamps, the lamplighter having earlier done his rounds with a tall ladder. We supped at a pie and mash shop and, taking into account Mrs Vernon's complicity, drew up plans.

"We owe it to Toddy at least," I said emphatically, pushing aside my plate, "to get that place shut down."

"I do not want the official force mobilised at this juncture, Watson. The infirmary business will be looked into. So far, we deduce the blackmail money, a considerable sum of 2,000 guineas, was transferred from Leytonstone to Hob Lane workhouse. The institutional establishment provides a link. We know certain of the inmates are being altered to become channels; the late Mr Price, even in his destitute condition, willed, for goodness sake, to bally well chuck himself in front of Anthony Sterling's chaise, all for the expedient of handing over a blackmail demand.

That is surely extreme. By the way, have you your service revolver handy, my dear Watson?"

"I have it here," I answered with some venom. "And it shall be the devil's own job to prevent me from blowing Dr Booth's brains out. The cur is a disgrace to the medical profession, his ethics intolerable."

"Stay your hand," insisted my colleague, giving me a timely word of caution. "Even with Lestrade's duplicity, it should be the devil's own job to get you off a murder charge. I should hate to have to attend your trial latterly when the judge puts on his severe black cap."

"Alright, but I shall say it again. How many more old fellows are destined to be fitted with electrodes? Are we to treat Mr Price and his ilk as mere statistics – collateral, and have done?"

"Of course not, but we must also consider whether Major Churchward and his associates have by now managed to replace the generator we destroyed at the factory with a new one."

"I expect they have, Holmes."

After our meal, we headed to a local hostelry to while away the time before we attempted our break-in at the poorhouse. Sherlock Holmes made excellent use of these few hours, chatting to punters in a casual way. One of them, it turned out, was an engine driver, a Mr Hay.

"The gasworks and the rubber processing factory are connected to the main line, you see, sir. The gasworks is the single largest user of coal in Horditch, closely followed by Kamens. Both have our own engines, Mary and Susan, industrial locomotives, built by the Avonside Engine Company of Bristol. They serve the yards well."

"Coal, of course, but I suppose useful for other goods," said my colleague, puffing on his pipe, nursing a half of Old Worthy. "Aye, like tonight. I'm told there's a special consignment, a crate or summat, early hours job, to be shunted from a siding; it's round the clock work for us."

"Shifts."

"Indeed, the yards can get quite busy of a night."

Buttoning our coats, seizing our hats and sticks, it was soon the hour to head outdoors, quitting the warmth and conviviality of the corner public house. A miasma of fog aided our cause considerably. Holding our bearings, we soon encountered the familiar iron railings along the pavement fronting the main building, 1866 – Hob Lane Workhouse etched into a framed granite plaque above the locked entrance.

Taking advantage of the strict institutional routine adhered to by London workhouses, we reused our previous route and crept round by the vast dustbins, making good use of the unattended door. Moving through the kitchen block, we exited at the large laundry room and, passing down a corridor, one of a number of connecting dormitories, we observed a few remaining attendants; women wearing caps and striped Worsted dress uniforms circulating amongst prone inmates who, at their customary bedtime, were allotted one of a row of coffin-like compartmentalised units running the whole length of the ward.

Suddenly, there was movement, the swooping of an eagle-eyed matron. A pipe was confiscated, causing one old fellow to sit up and elicit a volley of oaths against a certain Mrs Vernon, but he was firmly reprimanded, grudgingly sinking back beneath his blanket, she and other orderlies dimming gas jets, soon withdrawing to staff quarters.

Further up, on the ground floor, was a committee room lit by gleaming gas star chandeliers, a meeting then in progress. Holmes drew my attention to a partly left-open door, also an oblong plate glass partition window allowing us, while keeping a look out, to eavesdrop on proceedings. Likened to occasionally wavering candle flame, the forms of Lizzie Stride, Mary Ann Nichols and the other women of Whitechapel were sat around a table presided over by the more substantial plasmic entity of Maximilien Robespierre, Major Churchward himself about to chair a heated discussion.

Kelly, on behalf of the re-embodied spirits, proved a vehement spokeswoman. "You must, now the machine is ready, lose no time in plugging in the derelicts," she argued, "but Dr Booth, we require, I think, more inmates this time. As you will have noticed, our shapes are starting to fade in and out. Oh, we're energised, right enough, but look how my left hand flickers. That is surely not proper. Robespierre seems the most permanently plasmic of us. Is that because of privilege – your position, Monsieur?"

The Frenchman appeared gaunt and evilly inclined, finding these feminine concerns tending to hysterics. "I, myself, warned you, ma chérie; you femmes overtaxed yourselves in your recent labours, non?

Unnecessarily visiting Handbury Street, dealing with he who was responsible for your serial murders, an act of vengeful slaying which I applaud, but so soon, too hastily after your transfiguration, bah! The exertion required would have depleted your reserves. You supernormals, you only have yourselves to blame."

Both sly and suspicious, Lizzie Stride also spoke up. "The workhouse inmates, we have plenty; over one hundred and fifty. It is up to you, Dr Booth, to perform your surgery, to increase your workload – not six, as before, but fifteen cabled into the generator, channelling life forces to activate our ectoplasmic form more rapidly, more substantially. Think of it – more transfers; we shall be able at least to banish these body shivers."

"We would not want your outline schematising too much, dissolution of the molecular structure is bothersome, but we are pioneers, remember," Churchward replied, I surmised acting as a go-between. "Well, Dr Booth, you've heard what the lady said – six last time, why not fifteen this?"

"I am the workhouse master in charge of this institution," said he, irritably. "I have a medical board, the Poor Law inspector to deal with. I am responsible for the casual and fever wards. I cannot simply operate to order, implant on an industrial scale. Six are ready and will have to suffice. We are not iron lamp post manufacturers in the infirmary. The procedures are fearfully intricate. Some of the derelicts die on me, expire on the table. If it were not for the visible cranial surgery, I could sell most of these unclaimed bodies to my old School of Anatomy at Downing College, Cambridge. A fee of thirty guineas is paid by the school plus payment for a coffin and carriage by train. This is my normal course."

Quite unexpectedly, a thigh length, Cromwellian, brass-buckled boot walked across the floor by itself, and jumped unaided up into one of the vacant chairs that creaked, the upholstery sagging slightly as the heel dug in.

"Ah, Matthew Hopkins, welcome," said the Major, totally unfazed. The cockneys, however, the women of Whitechapel, burst into unkind fits of giggles. "Witchfinder General, you made it perfectly clear in our last planchette communication that you naturally wish to complete your transfer and properly flesh out and solidify. I am delighted to tell everybody that the new generator is more powerful than the original prototype destroyed in the fire. Robespierre says you simply continue with the programme, Witchfinder General – Mary Kelly again!" the chairman sounded exasperated.

"I say it once more, Monsieur Robespierre. Why do you not fade in and out like us? Are you given personal access to the machine, receive favours, one of the privileged elite? Are we girls lesser?"

"Ladies, please! The new generator arrives early this morning at the Kamens yard by rail. Dr Booth assures us six human electrode inputs are ready at the infirmary. I promise to arrange a séance for tomorrow night."

"We must hurry, our ectoplasmic state is fragile," said Nichols. "Neither of you suspects arsonists or a saboteur was responsible for the fire that interrupted our last séance," she added.

"We've argued this point time and time again. The old generator malfunctioned. A prototype, it simply overloaded and blew up. The fire was dealt with efficiently and my company did very nicely from the huge insurance payout."

"But Sherlock Holmes, the consulting detective?"

"Will be too afraid to act, fearing a fresh kidnap attempt against this Mrs Hudson," said the major confidently.

"None of them dare forget I, Maximilien Robespierre, during the revolution. 'Le Terror', was well used to dealing ruthlessly with hostile agencies. This inquisitor wretch, Holmes, is nothing intellectually when compared to radicals such as Danton or Marat. I proclaim that when we are further energised and more powerful is the time to strike him down. Madam La Guillotine shall raise her blade once more, and voila, into the basket!"

"Cannot we schedule the séance for the afternoon?"

"I beg of you, be patient," snapped the major.

"But your favouritism towards the Frenchman," insisted Mary Kelly.

"I will not, cannot, be accused of nepotism, surely," said Churchward, wishing to conclude proceedings. "Monsieur Robespierre does not, and never has, to my knowledge, received preferential treatment. Your keen helpmate, Kay Vernon, will verify this."

"Really, I'm not so convinced," sneered Lizzie Stride, flapping her arms ridiculously, I thought at the time, peering through the partition window. But not so ridiculous, as it turned out, for born of the mounting tension, the simmering annoyance of the Ripper victims sat round the table, none, it appeared, liking the dominance of Robespierre. Her other Whitechapel colleagues joined in, waving their arms frantically as a sort of protest; their pliable ectoplasmic forms burst into five bickering, aggressive birds, noisily squawking starlings flying round the room, pecking and clawing at furnishings, their razor-thin bills long and curved, gouging into upholstery and curtaining.

"The fairer sex, I ask you," shrugged the major when safely outside the door, he and the plasmic Frenchman having escaped the worst of the ensuing pandemonium in the committee room, the wildly squabbling flight of starlings making mischief before changing back into women.

Due to this fracas, luckily, no one saw myself and Sherlock Holmes rush over and dive behind a trolley heaped high with pillows and blankets. We remained there, hidden in shadow, watching incredulously as the Parliamentarian boot, imbued with the spirit of Witchfinder General Matthew Hopkins, followed the two men out of the committee room, walking by itself down the corridor.

We managed to hurriedly quit the Hob Lane poorhouse without being observed by attendants or the matron. Thus outside, traipsing along the foggy pavement after my rightful outburst, my colleague was quick to outline his preferred strategy.

"What disrespect," said I. "That pompous Robespierre, so scathing of your achievements, your considerable reputation, comparisons with Danton; Marat, murdered in his bath, for goodness sake. Your French grandmother should turn in her grave."

"My dear Watson, loyal you are, yet despite bluster, Robespierre and the supernormals are sublimely vulnerable. Correct me if I am mistaken, but if the new generator were to fail or, better still, be utterly destroyed, the spirit entities will dissipate, be bound to return to wherever ... absolutely done for."

"Why, yes, Holmes," I answered gleefully as we crossed the road. "The only possible outcome, for we learn their ectoplasmic force is already waning and requires replenishment. Even Robespierre surely would only have a limited span left to him."

"Then, old chap, cast your mind back to our conversation at the corner hostelry. A Mr Hay, the engine driver at Horditch gasworks. I recall you bought him a pint of Charrington's bitter."

"By Jove," said I. "Mr Hay told us himself. Some load awaits in a siding at Bow. The locomotive from Kamens to later propel it back to the factory yard. Churchward, likewise, mentioned a delivery early this morning."

"Hay is working the night shift. He and the rubber works engine driver are acquainted and knowledgeable of each other's work roster. His little gasworks loco, 'Susan', could prove most efficacious in speedily transferring us up the main line. Best foot forward, Watson, I observed upon the workhouse clock it is yet ten past one of the morning. We may, with the aid of a hefty bribe, yet outrun the Kamens engine by judicious emptying of our wallets, be first past the winning post. Horditch gasworks it is, then. Hup, hup!"

13

Before we find ourselves in more open country, East London's Victoria Park situated upon our left, the extensive Hackney Marshes on the other side, we come to Bow Station.

Travelling upon London & Blackwall company metals serving, amongst others, the parishioners of Shadwell, Limehouse, Poplar and Stepney, it being late few trains were running and by following a clear pattern of signals at Bow, our puffing gasworks engine came to rest in a short siding along by a boundary fence.

Even in the relative gloom we could perceive from the vantage of the train's cab a single goods wagon at buffers awaiting shunting.

"Well, Mr Holmes," asked our conspiring train driver, wiping his forehead with a damp rag. "Is it your idea to hitch the wagon up, take it elsewhere than the rubber works for the police to inspect?"

"Now, Mr Hay, discretion be the watchword. Scotland Yard shall indeed be privy to events, but for now, I shall require shortly a shovel full or two of red-hot clinker from your splendid firebox," directed Holmes, peering into the darkness. "For added insurance, after Watson has blown open the sliding panel of the stationary van with his service revolver, and I have made a brief explanation of the inner workings of the electricity generator, you will please, once we have leapt down, simply spread the flaming coals inside, the goods van's dry, wooden construction acting as kindling going far to create an eventful bonfire. We, I hasten to add, will be well on our way to Stepney by the time the fire takes hold."

Clambering down the cab steps, Holmes strode resolutely round the front of the engine from whence he plucked a large bullseye lantern from its lamp hook positioned on the buffer beam below the smokebox door. This allowed us enough light to see by.

At my companion's request, I aimed and fired my revolver, disposing efficiently of the locking device. Pocketing my gun, I beheld, in the gloomy interior, a machine well known to us. The widening glow provided by the bullseye revealed a large, black, steel box on casters, dials and switches and a main lever apparent, the generator stabilised by wooden blocks and securing ropes to the wagon's flooring.

"Your brandy flask, Watson," said my friend, crawling in, taking out his trusty pipe knife to unscrew one of the back panels.

"I see you have your own flask handy," I answered, noticing he had retrieved his own from his pocket.

"I must be quite frank, Watson. Back at our digs, I took the liberty of filling both yours and mine with a solution of dangerous chemicals; separated, the properties remain entirely benign."

"Chemicals!" I blustered. "But Holmes, I could have taken an impromptu swig, I might have casually this afternoon swallowed from the ..."

"But you did not imbibe, old fellow," he retorted. "Pray, be attentive, watch as I pour a quantity from my own brandy container over these bare copper coils, the mass of complicated wires. Nothing occurs, of course, but by adding a liberal measure from your own silver-engraved flask, by Jove, we obtain a reaction."

Sure enough, while acrid fumes stung my eyes and throat causing me to retch, the chemicals combined proved lethally corrosive and ate through metal like butter.

"Next time," I choked, dabbing my weepy eyes with a kerchief, "have the goodness to warn me when you purloin my brandy flask for such purposes," said I, much aggrieved.

"Ah, Mr Hay is stepping this way with his first fiery shovel of heaped clinker. I think, my dear Watson, we had best depart swiftly as, hopefully, will those pesky plasmic beings when no continued revitalisation is possible.

"Inspector Lestrade shall be alerted forthwith, for a police raid upon the Hob Lane infirmary is long overdue. And Mrs Vernon and Dr Booth have much to answer for."

14

I confess I am surprised at my industry, and shall allow myself the satisfaction of writing a very brief account of a case which I had fairly copied out in my notebooks, and still possess, but which, due to the laws of criminal libel governing usage of names of persons still living, has remained until now extinct from the public domain. My colleague, Mr Sherlock Holmes', love of the science of deduction is well known – the process by which he could, even from a very brief abstract theory, solve the most puzzling of crimes, a science that gradually predominated over every other taste. How great was his joy when a solution occurred to him – how despondent and low when there occurred a period of inactivity, and, alas, there was no case to solve.

Upon the morning of a gusty autumnal day at the end of October, following a night of gales, I heard a knock upon the door, and a personage entirely unknown to us, standing with bowler hat in hand, appeared at our rooms in Baker Street. He was a big man, with a square Teutonic head that could have been carved from a block of granite, a large-boned and heavyset jaw, and dressed very smartly: clipped hair and side-whiskers, long- tailed jacket and stiff, starched white collar turned down at the edges.

He hesitated upon the threshold until at length was moved to say, "Shadwell, Lew Shadwell. I 'opes I h'ain't interrupting, gents."

Holmes smiled. "Come in, dear fellow, come in. Don't stand there out on the landing. You are a concierge, else a porter, at the Albany I perceive, for although you've dispensed with your smart uniform top hat and coat, you persist in wearing a pair of the most distinctive maroon trousers in the West End. The sharply-defined emerald green stripe is the giveaway."

My colleague bent forward agitating the flames of a somewhat subdued sea-coal fire with the poker, waving away intrusive smoke blown down the chimney by the wind presently howling along Baker Street.

"Mr Shadwell. Here, have a cigarette, draw a chair up to the hearth. Watson, be a good fellow and pour our breakfast visitor a cup of coffee. My, my, this wretched smoking chimney is a bind."

"I wondered if I might 'ave a word, Mr Holmes. I am, a porter at Albany. I emphasise our code is strictly no publicity, so we must needs be discreet."

"Perfectly proper," Holmes rejoined.

"Well, sir, a gentleman what lives in an apartment upstairs, 'set' as they are referred to by us porters and residents, a Mr Ethby Sands, has not been seen or heard of. I took the liberty of opening his rooms this morning and, with your permission, I shall relate certain disturbing details."

"By all means, Mr Shadwell. I recall, Watson, Ethby Sands was an M.P., an eminent Justice of the Peace, who sadly was forced to resign his constituency due to ill health. He inherited a good deal of money from his father's agricultural machinery business and owns what is judged the finest collection of stuffed red birds of paradise in the country."

"Yes, I read in The Times," said I, "that he, along with the Marquis of Anglesey, helped sponsor the explorer and naturalist Alfred Russell Wallace, on his voyage to the Indonesian spice islands, or Moluccas. Wallace financed his work by sending rare zoological specimens to an agent in London who sold them on to museums or wealthy collectors such as Mr Sands. He spent much of his time in the western part of Indonesia visiting Sumatra, Java, Borneo and Sarawak. That was between '54 and '56, I believe."

"Oh, them bootiful stuffed red birds of paradise are a feature of 'is set, sir. Keeps 'em in lovely glass-fronted display cabinets, does Mr Sands. But, if I may continue, with my first impressions of Mr Sands' set, unusually his wheeled chair, such a part of him since he became gravely ill, was stuck at angles in the hall, the rug being slung in a most slovenly way across the armrests, not like his valet Garson would approve of, Mr Holmes, so that's something out of character. Next, 'is red shoes are missin'."

"Might I congratulate you, Mr Shadwell. You are first rate in your observations. Pray, enlighten us further. For instance, were the valet's bowler and winter overcoat absent from the hall stand?"

"Well, that's the crunch, there's just no sign of Mr Garson the valet, or of his master. The set looked to be abandoned at short notice – coffee cups unwashed, beds unmade, but it's that bloomin' pair of shoes what worries me, gentlemen. The rules at Albany is no dogs, no children, no silly noise – and I have to be absolutely clear here, Mr Holmes, no publicity of any kind. My residents, some of whom are crown prices, members of the aristocracy, talented artists, top milliners, actors of distinction, would definitely frown upon their privacy being invaded by any pushy policemen nosing around disturbing the refined atmosphere. I mean, Albany is exclusive, wonderfully situ'hated in Piccadilly. We don't want no coppers, thank you very much. But, certainly Mr Sands' absence bothers me, but not to the point of wishing to contact the official force and risk offending residents."

"Discretion is assured, Mr Shadwell. From what you have so far told me, you obviously fear Mr Sands may have been criminally abducted."

"What else am I to make of it? Mr Sands is a most gregarious and engaging individual. He, or at least Mr Garson, should never dream of absconding like this, going off somewhere without h'informing us porters. Why, Mr Holmes, he has been a resident of Albany for more years than I care to remember. We are on most pleasant and convivial terms. I pride meself on being a trusted confidante of personages, famous or otherwise, who live in our exclusive apartment block."

"Quite so, quite proper. I comprehend the delicate situation this places you under. One further point,

Shadwell – you are certain, in consulting with colleagues, that Ethby Sands and his valet Mr Garson on no account left Albany by the front entrance or via the Rope Walk?”

“Positive – but that's just it, you see, the red loafers, Mr Sands has been ill for some time,suffering from a wasting disease that has left him very weak and reliant on his valet for everything. He would be incapable of walking anywhere, even if he wanted to. He has been confined to a wheeled chair for the past six months.

Allowing Mr Shadwell to make his own way by subterranean railway, holding onto our hats, we hailed a hansom outside our diggings and, with a persistent sharp wind, it being very cold in London, there had been a flourish of sleety rain the previous day, our cab was soon rattling down Old Bond Street, my companion wholly concerned with checking his leather pocketbook, for it turned out we had an appointment at Fortnum & Mason's restaurant to share a pot of tea and cakes at the invitation of our theatre friends, the impresario Langton Lovell, and his business partner, Charles Lemon, the acclaimed actor. A dazzling new musical, a light opera, was on the horizon and they were anxious we should meet both the composer and lyricist responsible for writing the new production, which would be having its opening night at the Wimborne Theatre in Drury Lane. We occasionally dined with Lovell and Lemon at Goldini's, else Simpson's-in-the- Strand, and had known them for a number of years.

Albany, that most stately of Georgian piles, situated so conveniently in the heart of Piccadilly, a stone's throw from the grandeur of St James, is a bastion of privacy. The inhabitants guard the tenure of their selective sets with alacrity.

"My brother Mycroft lived here for a time," remarked Holmes, faintly smiling, putting his pocketbook away as our cab drew up outside the main entrance.

"Did he, indeed?" said I, surprised by my friend's revelation concerning his portly brother. "The exclusivity, the monastic bachelor ambience, the nearness of Fortnum's, Burlington Arcade, within walking distance of St James, or the Houses of Westminster – all this appealed to him wonderfully. Mr dear Watson, surely it is no secret that the 'picky' board of trustees who oversee this establishment show favouritism towards members of the Diogenes Club when a set becomes vacant for occupancy. Ah, Mr Shadwell, lead the way."

After we had been shown the Rope Walk, we hurried through the main entrance with its imposing pedimented facade, then along the central corridor adorned with busts, including a fine representation of Lord Byron, to a staircase whither was situated the set in which Ethby Sands resided, or at least should have resided.

"Last summer, Mr Holmes, you always saw Mr Sands in that little ivy-clad garden we saw earlier, sunning himself by the bronze statue of Antonius. It was his own little space. Mr Garson was always so attentive to his master and would keep him amused with observances of life in and around Piccadilly when out shopping."

"Most commendable. Could you let us in, Mr Shadwell?" Holmes asked. "Time is moving along, you know."

"Forgive my rambling so, let me just put the key in."

With the door open, it was surely that abandoned wheeled chair with the untidy rug thrown over it that seemed to admonish our intrusion, looking at us accusingly as if to imply 'he who it was sat on me once was murdered'. But Holmes paid little heed, bounding into the airy, tastefully furnished sitting room. There was a Chinese Chippendale chair, a linen Chesterfield sofa. Ming porcelain vases sat either side of the marble mantelpiece, and a gilt-framed portrait of Ethby Sands in the House of Commons hung above. In plain words, it was a bachelor's nest – comfortable and unfussy, books and a box of Coronas to hand, a japanned upright piano – which I pointed out to Holmes – standing in the bay. And, of course, a collection of stuffed red birds of paradise displayed behind glass and extending into other rooms in the apartment.

"A remarkable collection," I conceded.

The porter hurried out into the hall. "I last saw a pair of red loafers out there, Mr Holmes."

"He must be wearing them."

"But what use would they be to him, sir? He cannot walk. Like I says, he's stuck in a wheeled chair. Of late, his feet swelled up so bad 'e wore carpet slippers with toes slit like a turtle's mouth."

"A conundrum of footwear," chuckled my companion. "Now, Mr Shadwell, we do have a pressing engagement at Fortnum's tea rooms. You have already established that the valet's bowler and winter overcoat are absent from the hall stand, as are Mr Sand's gentleman's hat and coat – and scarf. Now, consider this carefully: did the ex-MP have a favourite walking stick, an ivory-handled cane, for instance?"

"Good 'eavens, Mr Holmes, now you come to mention, he used always to favour a metal-headed walking stick bearing a silver hallmarked ferrule. Would not be seen without it when out strolling along Piccadilly."

"But it is missing. A group of bamboo-handled umbrellas is all I see in the stand."

"Yes, it's gone, sir. Lor', I 'ope I haven't wasted your time, gentlemen."

"On the contrary, you were most wise to alert me to the possibility of some criminal enterprise, Shadwell. Do not fail to contact me again if Mr Sands fails to return to his set. Now, Watson, onwards to Fortnum's."

The blustery weather did not abate, rain expected later. We crossed the main road, then a brisk walk under overcast skies brought us to the famous emporium at No.181 Piccadilly. Passing through the opulent food hall, upstairs we found a delighted Langton Lovell and Charles Lemon beckoning us over to a table set for six persons. A waitress busied herself arranging the tea things.

Two people whom I did not recognise, one who had his face buried in a music score, the other charming and amiable, a cheerier personality altogether, were introduced to us as the lyricist Philip Troy and composer Christopher Chymes respectively, both working on a new musical, even now putting finishing touches to the score. They would be going on to a full-dress rehearsal later, it being less than a fortnight before the light opera was performed in front of an invited audience of guests and West End critics at the Wimborne Theatre. All concerned hoped it would become a smash box office hit. I learnt that Christopher Chymes was himself a resident at Albany, staying temporarily at the exclusive block of apartments because his father, when not abroad in Morocco, lived there.

"Yes, I know Ethby to nod to. I mean, none of us gets involved with small talk. We're all fairly reserved, respect each other's privacy, but I occasionally bump into him along the Rope Walk. Garson, his valet, is a gentleman's gentleman and a first-rate fellow. If I'm out along the arcade he'll invariably doff his bowler and stop for a chat. It's so damned appalling that Ethby is now confined to a wheeled chair. Old Garson tole me in confidence doctors have given up on him. They give him a month at most. Such a pity his parliamentary career got cut short. A human skeleton, 'rag bag of bones' is how he describes his master when out shopping in Piccadilly. Damned shame.

"Of course, I'm busy at my piano writing tunes, preparing the score. I want to hear that overture stomp, stomp, stomp and deliver such a catchy melody that all the audience will be up on their feet and clapping hands in under fifty seconds flat. Philip's written some amazing lyrics. He looks rather a miserable chap, but he writes the sweetest phrases, and of course when Langton and Charles read the music and words they immediately took us under their wing and we haven't looked back since."

"Ethby Sands – wasn't he a Tory M.P., or something?" mumbled Philip Troy, uttering only a brief pronouncement before disappearing behind his sheaves of script.

"Oh, and another thing, Dr Watson. I did, on occasion, see his collection of stuffed birds. He told me how Alfred Wallace managed to trap and kill them in

Indonesia. The natives are apparently very partial to the colourful feathers. Poor old birds of paradise, that's what I say. I mean, I doubt if there can be many left."

Of the pair, I judged Chymes the more outward going: charming and debonair, suited and booted by the finest Savile Row tailor, and Lobb for footwear. He wore an expensive men's fragrance. I should have hit on 'Floris', or 'Trumpers of Bond Street'. The fellow was a pleasure to share tea with.

Philip Troy, however, was silent and morose. He appeared to me buttoned up, unresponsive, preferring to sit and sip his tea, scowling at his pocket watch, else examining that score, anxious to get away to the theatre, see the first run-through, how the chorus sounded, so I shouldn't be too hard on the fellow. This was their first big break and I think he was on edge because of it.

Anyhow, promising Lovell and Lemon we would be there at the Wimborne on the big night, assuring them we wished every success with their new musical, we bid everyone adieu.

After bidding our theatre friends good day, we headed downstairs to Fortnum's food hall, which stocked a wide range of luxury goods. At the counter, we purchased packets of exotic tea, 'Gentlemen's Relish' and potted meats, and a boar's head in aspic jelly as a special treat for Mrs Hudson, who of late had been showing signs of disapproval after Holmes' late night chemistry, particularly the odour upon the upstairs landing that lingered for days without dispersing. My profuse apologies to our landlady on behalf of my wilful colleague had met with angry stares and I noted our normally first-rate breakfasts and suppers of late arrived cold, else undercooked – a broad hint that some mode of reparation was in order.

"Watson, do you perchance recall last Wednesday's edition of the Telegraph?"

"The rugby scores, certainly," said I.

"A Norfolk murder – it got barely a mention?" Our cab rattled round the Circus.

"Quite possibly," I now recalled the article headlined 'Grizzly death. Eel catcher horribly mutilated on the Broads. Norwich police baffled.' "You commented on it at the time."

"I received a letter this morning from Inspector Wells of the Norfolk force requesting that I should become involved in a consulting capacity. Incidentally, Watson, the official police surgeon, who remembers you studying at St Bartholomew's Hospital, insisted I be contacted, for the Norfolk murder bears all the exquisite hallmarks of a classic case, in which my peculiarly unique skills can be tested to the extreme."

"You sound like a blasted antiques dealer, Holmes, crowing about a fine piece of rare Ming picked up at some house sale. A human being is involved, who has family, remember."

"Be that as it may, we pack for Norfolk this evening, Watson. Leave early tomorrow morning. Your service revolver will be requisite for such an excursion into the wetland regions, the damp dreary climes of the Broads. Let us hope Mrs Hudson shall not serve up yet another inedible supper. Still, I think our handsome pig's head in jelly shall go some way to appeasing our redoubtable Scotch landlady."

According to Bradshaw's Guide, we were to travel upon the North London Railway joining the Great Eastern main line which would take us into the county of Norfolk, thence at Norwich we would change trains for a stopping service up the branch to Great Melchett Halt, whence the train continued up the single line to Cromer, that coastal resort renowned for its sea bathing.

A calmer, less blowy morning found us plumped upon cloth-covered seats lounging in a first-class smoker of the Norfolk Express, replete with a bundle of newspapers to help while away the long journey, plus a 2/6d lunch basket for refreshment.

"Time is of the essence," said Holmes, crossing his long legs, searching for his pipe and matches, sulphurous smoke from the locomotive in front wafting past our window as we departed King's Cross for the provinces. The morning was cloudy and overcast, a fine shower of rain splashing the glass as our train gathered speed passing beneath the gantry of signals.

"What of Ethby Sands, the missing chap from Albany? Does the case interest you sufficiently, or is it a dud? That porter, is he worrying unnecessarily? The theatre crowd didn't seem too both- ered."

"I grant you, the possibility of Sands being forcibly removed from his set appears slim, but that deuced wheeled chair left in the hall poses a conundrum. How can a fellow, who is supposedly gravely ill, with not much time to live and without the use of his legs, simply get up one morning and walk out of the door, his valet by his side? No, we cannot rule out foul play.

And then there's the queer matter of that missing walking stick and the red shoes."

"The what?"

"The singular metal-headed walking stick, his favourite – absent from the hall stand."

"Perhaps the blighter's bluffing, making out he's an invalid when in fact he's as fit as a fiddle, in perfect health – some insurance scam. It does happen, Holmes."

"Of course, Watson. If, however, it turns out he was abducted from his set under duress, I shall of course intervene. Have you a vesta handy, old man? I appear to have mislaid my matches." Travelling express upon Eastern main line metals, by mid-afternoon we had achieved Norwich in good time to change rains for the Cromer push-pull service.

"Ah, do you smell the pondweed tang of the wetlands, Watson? The Broads are not far off, our journey's end is in sight."

"What a wet and miserable day," I commented, gazing forlornly out of the window, considering the old castle upon the hill, an engine earning its keep shunting eight or so trucks laden with sugar beet into a siding. Whilst I pondered the gas works, a manure siding, the stacked timber, our compartment door was pulled open with a bang. Our guard, frowning in a most officious manner, held a form which he passed on to us.

"Another murder. I have been requested by our station master at Norwich, Mr Eades, to deliver this urgent telegraph message sent down the wires from Great Melchett signal box. You are the Mr Sherlock Holmes referred to here, I take it?"

"Here's a florin for your trouble, guard. A return message, take this down, inform your telegraph office to send the following reply: 'Inspector Wells, be with you on the one o'clock cross country service from Norwich, arrives at Great Melchett Halt 1.35 p.m. Require horse and trap. Sherlock Holmes.'"

The guard duly wrote down all Holmes had related with the stub of his pencil.

"A second murder, Holmes."

"Bears all the similarities of the first. By Jove, Watson, it appears the killer has struck twice. A grizzly murder, too! Perfect for occupying one's mind on a cold and damp afternoon, don't you agree?"

Our little two-coach train departed Norwich and proceeded to bustle up the branch northward towards Cromer. As our engine blew off steam, our carriages rattling over points, it dawned on me that we were quite possibly the only passengers on the train.

Holmes was eager to apply his clever brain to the case at hand. At length we drew into our station, just a basic waiting room and parcels office supporting a pagoda shelter.

Barely had we a chance to grab our luggage when there was a loud rap on the pane of the compartment window and we saw a great strapping chap with a florid complexion, wearing a soft cloth cap and plus-fours, about to open the door for us. This just had to be Inspector Wells of the Norfolk Constabulary. He helped us down. A little further along the platform, we encountered a dug-up flower bed edged in clay bricks, the name of the station displayed in whitewashed stones against the backdrop of the station master's runner-bean sticks. Beyond the end of the platform were a pair of level crossing gates and a fellow working the signals in his box. A porter, who barely registered our arrival, was stacking milk churns atop a trolley. The grey, lowering sky, the constant drizzly rain damping everything in sight, somehow offered a portent. This was no holiday jaunt, but a serious matter of murder, and I was impressed by the officious but polite way in which the detective welcomed us to this region of the Broads.

"Glad to meet you, I'm sure. Inspector Wells, up from Norwich. This is a grim business, gentlemen. It is a vile crime, and I must warn you the body discovered but a few hours previous by a local wildfowler is in pieces and being reassembled as we speak."

In no time we were rattling along in a horse and trap, being taken to the scene of the most recent murder at a lonely place on the Broads called Potters Ditch, where there was apparently a derelict windmill, long neglected and allowed to deteriorate, overlooking the channel.

"Walpole St Thomas lies that way, gentlemen," explained Wells. "The hamlet of Great Melchett is beyond the trees on the far side of that field of swede and turnip, and the road we are travelling on leads to Cromer. Unfortunately, I hear the North Sea is claiming the resort for its own and the cliffs are crumbling away."

To our right was the unending expanse of wetlands – reed beds that formed the famous Broads. All right in summer with the sail boats and holiday tourists, but this gloomy October the chilly dampness seeped right into one's bones.

"Its a determined fellow who poaches on these marshes of a misty evening," remarked Holmes.

"Indeed, what is there to interest the eye?" I remarked. "The deformed, windswept hedgerow tree, labourers' cottages. I have seldom seen a lonelier, more desolate terrain." I felt dampness on my clothes, my face cold and wet from the ever-persistent autumnal drizzle.

"The victim was using a coracle, you mention, Inspector?" enquired Holmes. "The shallow punt should have been more my preference."

"Ideal for stalking duck and other wildfowl for the pot. But this chap was checking his baskets, and it was during his inspection for eels that the ferocious attack occurred. Ah, we've almost reached the windmill at Potters Ditch. The sails, you will observe, were long ago dismantled. The place is in a sorry state of repair. A pumping station further up, the mill fell out of use long ago."

Once we jumped down from the trap and the horse tethered and fed his hay, we ambled across to the edge of a wide channel. A small island lay in the middle of lapping water, dark green and silted up due to the to-ing and fro-ing of the police officers in a row boat being ferried across to the island by a local wildfowler who was familiar with the area.

"The injuries are wholly consistent with a violent, swift attack by a person of great physical prowess who must be a clever swimmer," explained Wells. "The tidal flow is strong below the water. Misleading, as the channel appears calm, the surface of the water barely disturbed."

The police surgeon, whom I vaguely recognised from my time at St Bartholomew's as a fellow student, but whose name I could not for the life of me recall, came over and shook hands.

"Watson, isn't it?" he said, staring, making me a trifle uncomfortable. "Clayborne, Timothy Clayborne."

"Oh yes, I think you were in my year. This is Mr Sherlock Holmes."

"Glad to meet you, sir. This is a difficult case. Only last week, a little further along the channel, the remains of a headless body were found on the bank amongst the rushes. Do you want to share my flask of brandy? I can see our climate up here in Norfolk doesn't suit either of you metropolitans. In the autumn, we do get a lot of rain and mist. How are you bearing up, Watson? Like me, looking forward to a good dinner and a warming fire, I should wager."

"The pull of the convivial old country inn is very strong," I laughed. "Yes, I'm ravenous. Can you recommend a hostelry in Great Melchett where we can get a bed and board for the night, Clayborne?"

"The Duck and Drake is a warm and hospitable inn. They offer bed and breakfast and can knock you up a good meal at short notice. Isaiah Hooper is the landlord."

Clayborne drew back a blanket of sacking and Holmes and myself were confronted with a body much mutilated, torn about. My training as a doctor saw me in good stead, for a strong stomach is required on such occasions. The torso bore a distinctive tattoo – a 'hawk in flight' – across the broad chest which offered the best likelihood of identifying the victim.

"The body was found exactly where, Inspector?" asked Holmes.

The detective, wearing his gum boots, indicated to the island in the middle of the channel, as if floating in reeds. "A local wildfowler by the name of Hobtree, lurking hereabouts with his punt and gun, often uses the island as a vantage for bagging ducks. Scrambling up the bank concealed by rushes, he came across the remains. He is a local man and by the distinctive tattoo on the torso realised at once the body belonged to his compatriot Frank Peters, who is often at this time of year to be found eel-catching, setting up his baskets, baiting the pots."

"Capital! Observe, Watson, the overturned coracle clogged in the shallows. The island, you say – so the poor fellow was tipped out of the coracle and dragged across the space of water into the reeds. That would certainly require a strong swimmer."

"A swimmer of muscular characteristics, sir. The current is very strong – deceptively so."

"The channel must have been fearfully cold at this time of year?"

"Yes, a hardy swimmer, someone who managed to get that body – for the victim was not a small man, either, of light stature but well built and weighing in at I should say fourteen stone – across the stretch of water, up the bank and, in what must surely have been an unstoppable frenzy, killed Peters and fled the scene."

"By a punt or a coracle, I wonder? A row boat? The first Norfolk murder, if my memory serves me correctly, and I recall its geographical location from an article that appeared in last Thursday's edition of the Telegraph, occurred further along the bank where there exists a reed-thatched barn, more towards Dunham St Paul."

"That is correct. The headless body of George Flemps was found close by. But still we cannot fathom the physical nature of the perpetrator of that heinous crime."

"You infer an animal of some kind. Come now, Inspector Wells, we are in East Anglia – not the plains of Africa. No man-eating tigers or leopards in this neck of the woods. Nor is there, according to my pocket map, which I minutely consulted on our journey up here from King's Cross, any private sanctuary or public zoo in the vicinity of the Broads. Pray, what creature could have been large enough to inflict such injuries – a water rat, a vole, a mink? That really is a tiresome supposition. Might I venture to confirm – we are looking for a frenzied madman, a lunatic. You know, such people exist, Wells, and it is our job to hunt them down. I should like to amble across to the windmill and examine the location. Watson, be a good fellow and retrieve my tape measure and tweezers from your bag, old man. Still pining for a good dinner? Well, we shall soon be done with our sleuth-hounding for the day. The light is starting to fade, anyhow. See, the constables are gathering up Peters' remains on a stretcher. Clayborne, I see you're finished with the corpse for now and must be damned anxious to make an autopsy at Walpole St Thomas where the inquiry is based. Would you care to accompany us across to the windmill while there is still light?"

"I should be honoured, Mr Holmes. Your being here in Norfolk certainly livened up the local force no end. My own findings at present would concur with your lunatic theory. Who else could, with such physical strength and determination, swim across a strong current, dragging a body through the water during a particularly wet autumn which has seen severe flooding in these parts?"

"Just so. Now we make a closer inspection of the building. Your brandy flask, Clayborne, I have need of fire in my belly, for I'm chilled to the bone. My clothes are soaked through. A tipple for each of us is prerequisite to our foray across to that old windmill.

Hello! What's this?" My colleague's hawk-like features broke into a scowl. "Watson, you know my methods. Pray, what do you discern upon the path?"

"Holes, like the stumps of a wicket would make."

"The marks of a walking stick, old fellow, the ferrule embedded quite deeply in the giving ground of Potters Ditch – evenly spaced. Clayborne, I observed no police activity in this area. The muddy path is relatively undisturbed, is it not?"

"I noticed the police sergeant wander over here earlier, but he possessed no walking stick, or cane to lean on."

"Traces of the ferrule's point appear to lead from the direction of the windmill and all of a sudden cease. Of course, a harmless rambler cannot be ruled out. No signs of the paw marks of a dog in tow, though. We shall stroll across to that windmill, then it's dinner and early to bed at the Duck and Drake."

The mill was not of a wooden post construction, but rather a tapering brick tower with a tiny, framed window uppermost. Holmes' keen eye settled on the entrance door which had recently been defaced. The rain was falling hard and causing the ground to become even more muddy and waterlogged.

"This graffiti is recent. Observe the way in which the wood's whittled away by the blade of a sharp penknife, the impromptu carving exposing the lighter grain beneath. It purports to show the image of a large rodent. A penknife or chisel has been diligently employed, the artistry is really quite clever What say you, Watson?"

"I am in full agreement," said I. "This is no mere childish scratching by a bored youth." Inspector Wells, after supervising the removal of the body to a farm wagon for transportation to the village hall at Walpole St Thomas, had come over to join us.

"A rat. You know, gentlemen, there has been a spate of graffiti recently. The last week or so, 'Ratty' has been appearing everywhere, from telegraph poles to front doors, to defaced headstones. The local constable is being inundated with complaints, but no one is able to apprehend the rascal because this unconventional artist comes 'as a thief in the night', as the Good Book says."

"Be that as it may, Inspector Wells, I believe you should be aware that our murderer is possibly someone who uses a thin walking stick with a half-inch diameter ferrule. The marks appear to spread out along the path, leading away from the windmill, ceasing abruptly some ten yards or so distant from the edge of the reed bank."

Clambering over a five-barred gate, we trudged with difficulty across a claggy, arable field full of root crops, trusting to link with a footpath that led eventually to the hamlet of Great Melchett. The stack of the old sail-less windmill beside the waterway now a dark silhouette. As evening fell, I heard a locomotive whistle and was reminded of our two-coach train from Norwich with its crossing gats and box a mile or so distant.

"I must say, Holmes, the fatty tissue of the thigh appeared to me to have been gnawed to the bone. The victim's stomach was clawed open, leaving the intestines exposed."

"Ah, we are onto anatomy, eh? Well, old man, the throat was clean ripped out," Holmes declared as we turned onto our footpath.

"See the old manor house at the end of the

lane? Fifteenth century, I'll wager. It has gabled windows and pedimented stone arches."

We ordered our beer and boiled mutton in the snug of the Duck and Drake, a most charming country inn with a low, timbered ceiling, brownish yellow walls well seasoned by generations of smokers, heavy oak furniture, horse brasses and a homely log fire crackling in the settle of an enormous stone fireplace. We commented on the old manor and it turned out that Foxbury Hall, the property of Lord Astor, was, for the winter months, incredibly from September to March, rented out to Ethby Sands, who, before his illness, had been M.P. Of Norwich. A Brougham parked out front on the gravel drive.

"Mr Sands is very ill, gentlemen," said the landlord. "I've heard reports he is nearing the end and has not long to live. That'll be two-pence apiece for the beer and fourpence halfpenny for the dinner. Thankee kindly, gents."

"Thank you, landlord. Have you any tobacco perchance? A strong mixture?"

"Help yourself from the jar, sir. Do you require a clay churchwarden? The tobacco is on the house." "My charred old briar will be adequate for my needs, thank you, landlord, but I think another pint of the your excellent 'Old Worthy' is in order." We were about to return to the snug to enjoy our ale, smoke our pipes and take stock of events, when a clergyman, looking most perplexed and out of sorts, wandered into the hostelry. "Dear me," he snorted, "I fear this wretched unknown artist who holds the rodent population in such high esteem has struck again!"

"Aye," said the landlord, wiping a pewter tankard behind the bar. "I 'ears Miss Morley, the spinster at Crystal Cottage, reported her front door had been defaced, besmirched by black paint. Someone unseen and unknown, the culprit."

"How long must this sorry state of affairs continue? Another murder, I hear, over at Potters Ditch, and we have barely buried the first victim, poor George Flemps. It just wont' do. To be decapitated like that."

"Was the head ever found, vicar? They dredged the channel using nets the week afore last."

"No, Isiah, but dear me, please spare the gruesome details. I see we have two gentlemen present."

"Please sit down, padre," said Holmes, striking a vesta to light his pipe. "Might I order you a glass of sherry, or a cherry brandy? The air is so damp and chill at this time of day."

"Most kind. I am the incumbent here, the Rev. Marsden-Lee. I shall have a cherry brandy if you will. Oh dear me, this wretched outbreak of graffiti in our

Christian, law-abiding community has left me quite irritable and put out. Still, these things are sent to test one's faith, I suppose."

"Perhaps I could be of assistance," said Holmes, surrounded by a blue-tinged wreath of tobacco smoke. "I have some small experience concerning the dealings of petty crime." He chuckled whilst I drank the dregs of my Old Worthy. "I'm quite the puzzle-solver, you know."

"Well, I would be glad of some help, sir. It concerns the wall of my vestry."

"Your marshland church is 'decorated and perpendicular' – late medieval, I should wager," remarked Holmes as we crossed to the churchyard passing beneath the venerable lychgate.

"Oh indeed, we are fortunate enough to possess a much later painted window of thirty-four panels, its original glass preserved."

We traipsed round the side of the church and were presented with a round-headed arch above an oak door, weather-worn by centuries of lashing rain and mists seeping off the marsh of waterways and islands known as The Broads. Not long after, we stood in the vestry over by a cupboard where they kept surplices, appraising a caricature of a large rate boldly painted on the room's whitewashed wall.

"I am at a loss where to begin," exclaimed the clergyman.

"A puzzle easily enough solved. The mystery is already partly cleared up, at least," said my colleague with a bored air.

"Solved? You mean you have some idea who is actually responsible? Gentlemen, I am witness to a miracle. Pray, what on earth has prompted you to declare so easy a victory?"

"Here, on the stone paving, padre, and over there by the left of your desk – ah, and also beneath the encased vestry window, lie the dog-ends of cigarettes. It may interest you to know I have written a small monograph concerning one- hundred-and-forty known varieties of tobacco. The ash, I refer to. We are presently looking for a person addicted to hand-rolled cigarettes."

"Yes, I'm with you."

"Liquorice paper – so distinctive."

"Indeed, brown is the colour."

"Cork filters. Mark you, slightly stained with blood. Our quicksilver artist suffers from a chaffed, prominent upper lip, else bleeding gums. I rest my case. Do you, padre, recognise to whom I refer? If so, we have solved the identity of the graffiti artist in, let me see, under four minutes."

"Good heavens. I know to whom you refer. I recall the boy's incessant wilful smoking loitering about the graves on Tuesday last with some youths. Tommy Weekes. His gums are sensitive and bleed so that on occasions his front teeth appear bloodied and revolting. I must away to tell his mother of her son's disgraceful behaviour."

"Stay your hand for the present, padre. He is talented, I'll say that much for him."

"Talented! Really, sir, sacrilegious is how I should describe such scribblings. Oh, I realise the carvings and defacings do have a certain flair for the absurd. The giant rat drawn on Mrs Lacey's front door in her own image comes to mind. But he must be punished. A breech birth as a newborn, he was delivered by forceps and this has left him a little dull-witted. His behaviour is eccentric. Now I must depart and deliver the news to Mrs Weekes – that her son must go round with a cloth and pail and remove these images of rats from people's property. The carvings of rodents must, for the time being, remain."

"One moment, vicar," said Holmes in a concerned way. "I should like as reward to be the first to interview the boy and his mother. I would be interested, during a private interview, to witness his reaction to being found out. I promise all will remain confidential and I shall report my findings to you later this evening."

"That sounds fair. He lives with his mother at Thornycroft Cottage, a little way up the lane from my church. May I heartily congratulate you on solving this community matter with such elan and obvious professionalism. Your names, sir, so that I might recall this moment for prosperity."

"Dr Watson," said I.

"Mr Sherlock Holmes at your service."

"Good grief. Not the Sherlock Holmes?"

"Just so."

"Gentlemen, come to my rectory across the way at once. I must force a sherry on you both. I declare I am an out-and-out devotee of the Strand magazine and follow your articles avidly. Oh, and this evening you must join me for supper, I insist on it."

After a short stroll up the lane, banked on either side by tall hedgerow trees, we came across the lighted window of a cottage of thatched roof and cob, set some distance from the road. The vicar loaned us his bull's-eye lantern, for by now it was completely dark and visibility, due to the lack of street lamps in these country places, very sporadic, causing me to narrowly avoid tripping into a chicken coop as we approached the front door.

"Do come in, sirs. Would you like tea? There's plenty in the pot."

"Thank you, madam. A hot drink is most welcome on a bitter, rainy night such as this. We are new to the Broads and enjoying a birdwatching holiday. We're staying at the Duck and Drake further down."

"I will have a biscuit, thank you," said I, warming to the lady at once. She made us feel splendidly at home and seldom have I encountered such openness and genuine hospitality.

The labourer's cottage belonging to Mrs Weekes, a washerwoman by trade, who supplemented her modest income by sewing and mending lace and fabrics, consisted of a front parlour that, although cramped and smoky from the coal range, was kept trim and tidy and there was a homely welcoming atmosphere. Tommy, unaware that he was about to be unmasked and suffer reprimand for his art's sake, chomped on a thick wedge of crusty loaf smothered in dripping.

"Well, sirs, what can I do for thee?" asked the chubby matron, beaming with goodwill, her face lit up by the oil lamp above. "Help your'sels to more tea."

"We have just come from the rectory," said Holmes, taking out his pipe and tobacco pouch, placing them upon the chequered tablecloth, "where, before taking sherry, we were given a tour of the vestry by your most courteous and engaging clergyman, the Rev. Marsden-Lee. He was anxious to show us a new portrait he had recently acquired – somewhat simplistic and yet altogether a most well-orchestrated caricature. The face with its twitching whiskers stood out most particularly."

The boy, supping tea from his mug, went very bright red in the face and managed to spill scalding hot liquid down the front of his smock.

"Look at you, Tommy, you silly nitwit. What's come over you? Drink they'se tea properly like a young gentleman, like I'se always taught you as a good ma."

"I b'aint a nitwit," he fumed. "I'se cans't knock up a coffin, can't I? Shave the planks, French polish the elm to a grand finish?"

"Course you can, dear. Now don't get riled so. I know'st Simkins, our local builder and undertaker, is very pleased with your standard of work. He makes all the coffins for the villages her-abouts. He is of the opinion you are a skilful, worthy craftsman, but, like I says, don't slop tea everywhere."

"A craftsman in wood should be able to use a penknife, else a sharp chisel most effectively. Perhaps that old windmill at Potters Ditch could do with a plank or two pegged into place," remarked Holmes.

This time, the lad visibly tensed. Once more, his cheeks flushed, a quivering, nervous tic evident beneath his left eye. He scowled at my colleague, no doubt wishing he would disappear in a cloud of smoke up the chimney. He held his tea mug in a vice-like grip, so hard I thought his wrap-around fingers would crack the enamel.

"I shall be brief and entirely to the point, Tommy. I think you have considerable artistic talent and will go far. But the church vestry is hardly the best backdrop for you 'free-fall' masterpieces. Neither should you go round defacing headstones, else daubing paint on doors. You have left a trail of etched graffiti in your wake, my dear fellow. Youthful angst, a need to express oneself by defacing property, is hardly a new phenomenon. You are not the first young man to rebel!"

Tommy Weekes' jaw dropped. A withering sigh escaped his parted lips revealing diseased gums with a potential to bleed. He sat at table entirely undone, his shameful secret exposed.

"Fear not, the most you shall receive from this interview as punishment is washing down and re-whitewashing the vestry wall. Neither Dr Watson nor myself have any inclination to cause either yourself or your dear mother the slightest embarrassment. That said, I shall rest my case only when I have got to the bottom of why, on every occasion you choose to strike, the image is the same very time – a rat! An extremely large and ferocious rat! Apart from the matter of whitewashing the vestry wall at ten tomorrow morning, which you will perform as just penance to appease the wrath of the vicar, why I ask does the same restive image dominate your graffiti art? I put it to you, young man, something has upset you, some recent event infected your creativity. I believe you know who, or what, was responsible for killing the first victim, George Flemps, up by the barn."

"A rat!" he cried, bursting into sobs. "I see'd a giant rat, sir. Honest I done. I see'd it swimmin' along the Broads wi' my own eyes. I bared witness to it. I did see a giant rat wi' the head of George Flemps in its jaws, I did so."

———

By the time we had trudged up the lane to enquire at the hall over Mr Sands' health, it was pitch black and raining heavily. Fending off the worst of the inclement weather with umbrellas borrowed from the vicar's stock of 'lost and found', brollies forgetfully mislaid on pews of a Sunday by parishioners over the years, we wondered whether the ex-M.P. might have come down here on the train from London to take up residence for the winter season, forgetting to inform the porters at Albany of his whereabouts, perhaps with the use of a basket chair, a hired invalid carriage, causing him to leave behind his usual wheeled chair at the apartment. Holmes was pretty certain this was the case, and anyhow, the Norfolk murders were of more concern and we had a full day ahead of us as to the violent deaths locally. The exact whereabouts of Ethby Sands was really a secondary consideration.

We came to a set of gateposts surmounted by a pair of winged gryphons, thus continued up the path until the old clay-brick Norfolk mansion came into view. Foxbury Hall was, I was sure, in the sunlight of an autumn morning, an elegant home full of character and charm. Earlier, I had judged the architecture to be of the Elizabethan period. The gables, diamond-paned windows and tall herringbone brick chimney stacks gave the house an air of imposing grandeur.

Once inside the porch, I tugged the bell-pull, aware of dripping, gurgling rainwater pouring off the guttering. We waited expectantly beneath the hornbeam lantern for the front door to be opened.

Soon after, a genial fellow in frock coat, striped trousers and black tie greeted us. "My name is Garson, sirs. How can I help? The weather at this time of year is most uncongenial and bothersome. I used to always prepare my master's hot toddy at this hour, make sure he was comfortably seated by the fire with a shawl wrapped round his shoulders."

"Is Mr Sands at home by any chance?" asked my colleague. "I perceive you are his valet. We were just passing and wished to convey our good wishes. He is in, presumably?"

"I regret to say, gentlemen, condolences are in order, for my master passed on at six of the clock this morning. The wasting illness from which he had suffered interminably for the last year finally claimed his life. He just had no energy left to fight, sir. I trust you will respect the fact that the body of my master yet still resides in the house, we are all of us in a state of deep mourning. Goodnight, gentlemen, and Lord bless you for enquiring after Mr Sands at this sad time."

"That just won't do," my colleague remarked, showing grim fortitude as we walked back down by the shrubbery, hastening to the rectory to keep our appointment. "A chronic invalid should not be subjected to a lengthy journey from the heart of Piccadilly to north Norfolk during autumn when the air is damp and chilly, the region steeped in marsh mist and prone to continuous drizzle. Switzerland, or the Italian Alps are understandable, but East Anglia! Really, my dear fellow, as a doctor would you subject your patient to such unhealthy climes?"

"Absolutely not," said I, in full agreement. "In summer, the Broads offer sailing and boating to one's heart's content, genial hours spent at the tiller exploring the channels, but at this time of year bronchial infections, stiffening of the joints – a patient's chest in particular should be susceptible to pneumonia. If they are already weakened and not able to eat properly, such as Ethby Sands, no – the vaporous, tangy air of the wetlands for a long-term sufferer such as he, I should class as positively injurious to health."

Having kept our appointment, we were enjoying our evening meal. The Rev. Marsden-Lee invited us to share a repast of roast haunch of venison at the supper table in the oak-panelled dining room, prepared by his housekeeper. The candles, I confess, cast a somewhat eerie illumination on the portraits in oils of previous incumbents that were hung about the room.

"Dead!" The clergyman shrieked with laughter. "My dear Holmes, if only you had asked, I could have told you that much and saved you both a wasted journey. The matter of Tommy Weekes was, of course, uppermost in our conversation when we last spoke over sherry. I myself visited Foxbury Hall this afternoon after learning of our old Norwich M.P.'s passing. Most sad, but not entirely unexpected due to his chronic state of health. But, you know, it all went rather queer."

"What went rather queer?" said I, sampling a glass of excellent burgandy.

"We heard a rumour, a death up at the big house, Mr Sands' passing, of course. Well, Mrs Lunn, our ministering angel, who does the flowers in my church, a woman of advanced years who whenever there is a death in the village takes it on herself to prepare the deceased – washing, doing the necessary, sheeting the corpse, making everything presentable, by no means an interfering old busybody – came to me in floods of tears. A man up at the manor house had apparently told her to get off the property. He called her a witch!"

Holmes glanced up from his plate, his pale, sallow, aquiline features all aquiver from the wavering light of the candelabrum on our table which cast shadows about the room, making those dratted oil paintings of stern old country parsons seem alive and overly judgemental.

"Yes, I think we catch your drift, padre," said he. "The old lady was naturally upset by this fellow's uncouth attitude."

"I asked her if it was not Mr Garson, the valet, to whom she referred. 'Oh no, sir,' she insisted, 'for he is a gentleman, a man of impeccable manners who should never dream of addressing a lady like that. This was a young man wearing red loafers claiming to be the son.'

"'But, my dear lady,'" I replied, "'Mr Sands was a confirmed bachelor. He never married in his life and was, before his illness, fond of his clubs and fine dining. He was a fellow who, as far as I know, had no understanding whatsoever of the ways of a woman's heart. Garson was his only constant companion over the years, in good times and bad. A son? Why, that's absurd! I shall ask cook to make you a very hot gin and water while I meanwhile go and give this young bounder a good talking to!'"

"Bravo! Most commendable."

"I was appalled by the insensitive treatment of this woman who, after all, only wanted to help lay out Mr Sands with all the dignity and care she could muster, so I went to the hall, cutting through the walled kitchen garden, and saw the back door to the house had been left open. Well, I am acquainted with Lord Astor, who rents Foxbury Hall out in the winter, and know the layout of the rooms fairly well, so I let myself in and – what a shock – there was a group of Chinamen, I ask you, bickering with one another, consulting a map that had been laid out flat on the kitchen table, a map depicting the naked human form, indecent and covered in heretical symbols and underlinings, the diagram countenanced by numerals and Chinese letters of the alphabet. The abhorrent scent of powerful joss alerted me to Oriental mischief, wholly un-Christian ethics."

"Practitioners of alternative medicine," corrected my companion good-naturedly. "They were merely discussing acupuncture, studying a chart, my dear Marsden-Lee. I have spent time in Tibet and China and can assure you there was nothing untoward regarding their activities. Do carry on. Your observations are first-rate."

"Be that as it may, Mr Holmes, I demanded to see Mr Sands' body there and then, to view the corpse."

"Ha, ha, by Jove that's good and pushy."

"To offer up a prayer for the dead in the Anglican faith. Well, my arrival was greeted with polite disapproval. I was bustled away by their leader, a tall, gangly Chinaman, austere to the extreme with a cruel mouth and menacing airs who went by the name of Wu. Dr Wu Xing. He was evidently held in high esteem, for the other Orientals would respectfully bow when referring to this chart of blasphemy.

"I was evicted! Evicted from the hall as a trespasser. Me! The vicar of the parish and on friendly terms with Lord Astor. Well, I have not been back since."

"Did you, perchance, observe anything else of interest?" asked Holmes.

"Now you come to mention it, I was passing round by the shrubbery and happened to peer into the billiard room. The windows look out onto the flower beds, and the lawn and tennis courts. Well, I chanced upon the strangest thing, for there on top of the green baize billiard table was a most peculiar receptacle. Not exactly a proper elm coffin, more of a wicker compostable shell, a light- weight coffin of basketwork favoured these days by faddish vegetarians and slavish pre-Raphaelite followers of William Morris who prefer to be buried beneath a flower bed in the garden."

"And of the young man calling himself the son?"

"I saw nothing of him, Mr Holmes. He might well have been a complete stranger, an impostor, for all I know."

Inspector Wells called for us bright and early. We were ensconced in the snug of the Duck and Drake, eating our breakfast of ham and eggs, washed down by halves of warm beer, in front of a roaring fire in the settle. One only had to glance out of the latticed window to confirm it was a misty, damp morning – grey and overcast.

"An autopsy is to be performed over at Walpole St Thomas at nine of the clock, gentlemen. Dr Clayborne is anxious we should start on time. I have the horse and trap waiting."

"Heaven forbid that we should delay proceedings, Inspector, but I fear I and Dr Watson must return to London. There is at Albany in Piccadilly a mysterious disappearance which, for now, must take precedence over the Norfolk murders. After a brief walk to stretch our legs we will be departing for the station halt to catch the next London-bound train. My pocket Bradshaw indicates we shall be required to change at Cambridge."

"Well, I must say, isn't that highly irregular, Mr Holmes? What can possibly take precedence over two horribly orchestrated murders?"

"Finding the perpetrator, Inspector. What else have you to tell me?"

"Well, sir, we found an interesting item when dredging the channel at Potters Ditch – a muddied, stout ash stick, more of a cudgel – handle of curved antler."

"Then I suggest you check locally who might own it! Landlord, a fill of your most excellent tobacco from the jar. Please prepare our bill, for we shall be leaving presently."

I can report, upon our return journey to Norwich, both of us were avidly reading the first editions of the daily papers, the pages of which were spread over the cloth-covered seats, little was said.

My dear friend, his briar-root pipe clenched between teeth, was smoking contentedly, filling our compartment with the reek of coarse country inn tobacco. I tamped down strands of my own preferred Arcadia mixture into the bowl of my pipe and struck a match, glad to be leaving behind the dreary scene of the Broads and returning to Baker Street.

We caught an express at Cambridge and, as we rattled along, Holmes, as he was wont to do, while scowling at the obituary notices, proceeded to underline a section of print with his propelling pencil, passing me the folded newspaper. I was thus able to become further acquainted with the life and times of Ethby Sands, once an M.P. for Norwich, who owned a fabulous collection of rare, stuffed birds of paradise and had also, notably, composed a best-selling hymn tune.

There was the proper mention of his final days, the enduring struggle against the virulent form of wasting disease, and the correspondent ended with 'Died peacefully in the early hours with his beloved valet, Mr Henry Garson, by his bedside at the country seat of Lord Astor in the county of Norfolk'.

"A complete and utter fabrication, my dear Watson, cleverly placed in this morning's edition of the Telegraph. No doubt all the broadsheets bear testimony to his life ... and death. His admirers shall genuinely mourn his passing. His detractors wholly welcome it."

"Detractors? Who are they?" I asked.

"At present I am not at liberty to say. Once we have returned to the capital, might I bother you to accompany me to the Royal Geographical Society in Exhibition Road?"

"Certainly," said I, continuing to stare out of the compartment window.

The fog lay thick, dun-coloured, blanketing the metropolis, making visibility poor and our journey across London from the station slow as to be almost futile. East of the Albert Hall, it took us ages to reach the Royal Geographical Society. We were stuck in a jam, with carriage, omnibus and dray traffic virtually at a standstill.

"Why on earth are we visiting the R.G.S.?" said I, while our cab rattled up Exhibition Road and our goal was at last in sight, the familiar red-brick Queen Ann facade coming up on our right. "I have seen no lectures advertised. Drat it, Holmes, I should have preferred to spend my time as an idler perusing my latest edition of the British Medical Journal before the hearth."

"I have in mind a rather pressing matter concerning old maps and logbooks."

"Old maps, logbooks? I don't follow."

"I am curious to delve more fully into the matter of the island of Sumatra."

"Not those blasted stuffed birds of paradise! Really, Holmes, you are the limit!"

Cedric Bitten, long-serving secretary and senior librarian, an epitome of jolly eccentricity, brimming with fascinating information, led us into the map room. He proved most civil knowing both Holmes and myself by sight, for we attended various exhibitions and lectures over the years, including those of David Livingstone and Fridtjof Nansen, the Norwegian explorer.

The frock-coated gentleman, half blind from years of study as an Oxbridge don, wore the thickest-lensed spectacles I ever saw. He beckoned us to a table and awaited Holmes' request with great patience.

"My dear Bitten, I am indebted to your unsurpassed knowledge of travel books and maps. This sounds trite to the extreme, and I must profusely apologise for such a nonsensical waste of valuable scholarship, but have you, in your long experience as R.G.S. L;ibrarian, ever come across the image mark of a rat?"

"Gabriel Doppelmayer's celestial chart of 1742 shows a curious rat and we do possess an early sixteenth-century Portuguese map which depicts a caricature, a replication of a giant rodent positioned above one of the remote Indonesian islands, or Muluccas, as is their proper title."

"Sumatra," said I, hardly believing my ears. "Sixteenth-century, you say?"

"Just so, Dr Watson. Be good enough to wait here. I shall ask young Credon, our junior clerk, to fetch the appropriate folder from the rack. Would either of you, perchance, like a cup of coffee? It is devilishly foggy and your journey from the terminus fraught with delays at every turn."

"Most kind," replied Holmes. He warmed his hands in front of the vast ornamental mantelpiece, a crackling fire in the grate. Paintings in oil of famous explorers and past presidents of the Society graced the oak-panelled walls.

Our genial librarian shuffled off to fetch coffee.

"You know, my dear Watson, Bitten is really a most amazing fellow. His brain is quite the finest storage facility for facts concerning geography and antiquated travel books, logs and documents I have yet to come across. I am not saying he is on par with brother Mycroft, who possesses the most retentive brain attic in all England, able to analyse and store myriad facts and figures and details of minutiae, but Bitten is close

– damn close. Ah, thank you, Credon. Here, Watson, our map has arrived, neatly bound in tooled green Morocco, I perceive."

Holmes raised his magnifying lens and together we leant over and carefully studied this very old and rare coloured map of the tropics.

"We have it, Watson, we have it!" my colleague said at length, excitedly seizing my arm. He was jubilant, for there, drawn across one of the beautifully colour-tinted islands was clearly a ferocious looking rodent of massive proportions – a terrified native Sumatran clamped between its bloody jaws, filthy, sharp incisors buried into the poor fellow' neck. He was to be devoured while other natives looked on, surrounding the giant rat brandishing primitive spears and a net.

Bitten returned with our refreshments. "Might I just mention in passing, gentlemen, the word 'giant' is but a loose generalisation. The proper translation is 'great and munificent'. Thus, you can infer from this illustration that the native population not only hunted this rodent, but also revered it."

Bitten passed us each a cup of coffee from the tray. Thereafter, craning his neck and refocusing those pebbly lenses he commented with obvious disdain,

"Peculiar creature – represented as a carnivore, a man-eater. Tut, tut, really, that is taking liberties."

"The ears are certainly longer and hairier than the common black rat that so infests our London sewers," I remarked, sipping my coffee.

"Yellow, gingery fur, mottled to form patches of white, Watson!" said my colleague enthusiastically.

"Now, now, gentlemen," warned Bitten, "you must proceed delicately. You, Mr Holmes, are speaking as though 'Ratty' here were real, that the species actually exists. This just won't do. The trained cartographer would regard this caricature with justified scepticism." He paused to take a sip of coffee. "Map artists in the sixteenth-century were notoriously inaccurate and took untold liberties."

"In this instance, I'm not sure the illustrator did not get it exactly right," said Holmes, a worried expression surfacing on his hawk-like features. "Now, on to the printed word, Mr Bitten."

"Mr Holmes, I have already instructed young Credon to extract from the library shelves a number of suitable volumes – naval documents recording early voyages to the spice islands, copies of course, the originals being way too fragile to handle."

Credon duly provided the aforementioned documentation. One extract from a logbook belonging to a Captain Dreyfuss Malmby R.N., particularly caught our interest. Written in brown, watery ink with a quill pen, each page meticulously recorded an expedition by a group of officers and ratings who first came ashore to the island of Sumatra in a row-boat armed with pistols and muskets, evidently fearing the worst. But those fears proved ungrounded.

Our vessel safely anchored in the bay. Upon landing on the island named Sumatra, I am thus gratified to report no hostility did we encounter, rather the natives appeared both friendly and industrious, eager to trade for a variety of fish, fruit and much- prized spices, in exchange for tobacco and iron cooking utensils. A peculiarity upon which we all remarked was the fact that not one old or ailing person did we encounter. Even in the village of palm huts it appeared age and infirmity had been banished, for no old people were to be seen, neither sleeping, cooking, nor going about their business. Village elders, so much a part of Indonesian culture, the mainstay of a community, were entirely absent. I thus congratulated the chief amongst this tribe of young men and women through a translator, and heartily commended the health and well-being thereof. Grinning, he pointed to a cooking pot and flayed animal skins drying out, hung from poles. These rough, hairy hides were evidently precious to them.

Our initial fears were that the old and infirm were, at a certain advanced age, led away to a jungle clearing and left to be devoured by predatory beasts as in certain other tropical cultures. I was assured that, by consuming the flesh of a giant tree-rat who inhabited this island exclusively, youth and vitality were maintained and that bones of that same animal, when ground down to a fine powder, enabled a man or woman to live to be three hundred years of age, and that most of the islanders had never known a day's illness in their lives, the average age being two-hundred-and-fifty years.

The meat, I doth report to my king, be tough and inedible, though sampling a sip of the special potion they talked of, the effects upon the bowels were most agreeable and filled us with a sense of well-being and wonder at our situation.

Ratings and officers alike, we rowed back to our sailing barque in good spirits with eight natives palm baskets brimful of spices.

Ship's Doctor's Report: H.M.S. Bulldog

After a most thorough examination, ratings and gentlemen officers alike, I confess, dear brethren, I am at a complete loss to explain exactly how the older ratings (indeed, our Captain himself is nine- and-fifty years of age) seemed verily sunnier and full of much youthful exuberance. Their physical ailments and grumpy demeanour so evident before their departure in the row-boat replaced by muscular suppleness, youthful faces, and they are so jolly and overbearing as to cause me great displeasure.

The ratings and officers I examined showed signs of increased vitality and strength since visiting the island called Sumatra. Am I, a man of science, to wholly support such unnatural change in a man, else, as I suspect, some diabolical, un- Christian sorcery may be at work?

"What are we to make of this, Holmes?" said I, placing my coffee cup back on the tray in a state of continuing puzzlement.

"The evidence mounts up, my dear fellow," said Holmes with a frown. "It is obvious to me, Ethby Sands has given himself over to some dastardly medical experiment. His absence from Albany, the time spent in Norfolk, bodes ill."

"You infer this group of Chinese, led by Dr Wu Xing, the alternative medicine crowd, may have succeeded in producing a viable serum that duplicates, in modern terms, the effects of the native potion of powdered bone?"

"I do, Watson. I do, old man. Come, we must make haste in a cab to the telegraph office. There is a person who, above all others, can enlighten us further concerning this peculiar case."

I recall, as if yesterday, a slender, tall gentleman with nut-brown complexion, sporting a long bushy beard and round wire-rimmed spectacles entered our rooms at Baker Street. He had been guided up the stairs by Mrs Hudson, who I could see was in complete awe of our visitor, and with good reason, for here in our modest bachelor apartment were host to the explorer and naturalist, the author of The Malay Archipelago, Alfred Russell Wallace – he, who had been a close friend of Darwin and, at great cost to his own health and personal finances, single-handedly explored some of the remotest islands on earth.

It was a rare privilege indeed to receive his Panama hat and brolly and, once he was comfortably seated before a blazing fire in the grate, Holmes poured us each a glass of whisky. My colleague arranged this interview with the great man at short notice, Wallace being down in London for the opening night of the new light opera at the Wimborne, Drury Lane, written by the lyricist Philip Troy and composer Christopher Chymes.

We had, ourselves, been invited and were fortunate enough that same evening to attend, sharing a box with Wallace, his wife Annie and their daughter Violet and sons Herbert and William, who had come up from Cornwall especially, staying at the Langham. Holmes refilled his pipe and, languidly stretching his long legs across the bearskin hearthrug, posed his first question.

"I recall noting in your autobiography, Wallace, that you went down with a serious fever some time in 1858. You nearly lost your life due to malnutrition and the onset of a severe strain of malaria. You lay on your cot drifting in and out of consciousness for many days and nights, but you received an unusual visitor, a shaman from the Indonesian island of Sumatra."

"To an explorer in the tropics, Mr Holmes, the unseen dangers of semi-starvation and disease are always present. I was, at the time, you will recall, lying on a cot-bed in a palm-thatched house, dangerously ill, hallucinating. My feeble constitution unable to stave off a virulent bout of yellow fever. I must emphasise, gentlemen, that had it not been for the intervention of this native shaman, I believe I should have died, been lost to hoards of black ants, giant centipedes and carnivorous termites who abound in that region of the interior, and certainly never made it back to England alive."

"A shaman, you say," said I, taking notes in my little pocketbook.

"Indeed, Dr Watson, I had long known the Albverro of Seram, for instance, were renowned and powerful magicians and spirit guides. But it was a bird trader of all people with whom I had been doing business, who happened to be visiting Sumatra and, using all his influence, persuaded this powerful shaman (for a substantial consignment of rare bird feathers) to travel across the islands on a trading prahu and visit me. So there was I, suffering dysentery and a high fever, sweltering in that damn palm hut, when this kindly native shows up. I barely registered his presence at first. I recall a happy, dusky fellow patting me on the shoulder, allowing some sweat from my brow to trickle into a tiny clay pot he kept strung around his neck. My native visitor lost no time in assessing my condition and it was lucky he acted so promptly. From beneath his shawl, he drew out a bundle of brittle old bones wrapped in the stiffened, mummified hide of some long dead animal. A horribly squashed head, large furry ears, a compressed snarling snout – the vilest looking, longest and sharpest incisors I ever saw. The acute smell of the matted fur, the leathery skin, repulsed me.

"'Take it away,' I exclaimed, more dead than alive. 'Take the damn thing away and burn it.' The native, emitting a chuk-chuk-chuk, chuk- chuk-chuk from between pursed lips, seemed to soothe my fevered thoughts, calm my inner being wonderfully. I slept soundly for the first time in weeks, awaking to find my new friend, my surrogate mother, if you will, squatted on his haunches, busily occupied with pestle and mortar, grinding bony fragments from that awful emasculated creature into a fine powder which he then placed in a jar and mixed with a quantity of blood drawn by hideous slug-leeches cleaving to my inner thigh, to form a mash to which he added water. The shaman would allow me to sip of this potion."

"This animal, would you classify it as a rat?"

"Why yes, Mr Holmes, a giant tree-rat native to Sumatra, a species rare and long extinct. I grant you, I regarded the specimen as a valuable link in the evolutionary chain. At the time, my dear friend, Charles Darwin, was busy embarking upon his great work On the Origin of Species, and perhaps if I had been more my old self, I would have drawn his attention to the giant Indonesian tree-rat. As it was, I loathed the sight of the filthy- smelling vermin. However, gentlemen, when it came time for Samu, the shaman, to leave, and I was fully recovered, he left the skin and bones for me and I had not the heart to throw them out or destroy them. So Samu, that dear, beloved companion of mine for so long, left me the tree- rat remains as a present – a gift to recall our association. They got placed in a bamboo crate and were all but forgotten, until my eventual return to these shores. It was only when I began to classify and label my finds back in London, and by this time I was happily married, that the old bones, wrapped in animal hide, once more came to prominence. I recall my darling wife found the items stuffed behind one of my portmanteaux. She picked up the rolled-up carcass of matted hair and calcified bone, commenting about the awful snout and teeth. 'I don't care if it's a rare Sumatran tree rat, Alfred, for goodness sake get rid of it. The old skin and bone pong's to high heaven and should be heaped on the bonfire. I don't want it in the house. I dread to think what formidable mites and ticks it is host to.'

"Of course I did not want to destroy the specimen, so we contacted Charles Darwin and his wife and they agreed to take it off my hands."

"Now we come to the crux of the matter, Wallace. We know much about your giant tree-rat of Sumatra, but next to nothing about the potion. Another whisky?"

"I will have another, thank you, Holmes. All right, the potion. Well, I can honestly say, hand on heart, it worked. If there is such a thing as the elixir of eternal youth, this gets damnably close. Not only did it contain healing properties, but when I next looked in the glass after being confined to my cot with yellow fever, I had lost my middle age and become young again. I felt cleansed, entirely rejuvenated in both body and mind. Samy, the shaman, insisted he had lived three hundred years, and amongst his tribe on Sumatra he was but a young man, a mere whipper-snapper."

"But, scientifically, surely that's unfeasible – an anti-ageing potion belongs to Greek myth," said I, stubbing out the remains of my cigar in the ashtray.

"Make of it what you will, gentlemen," said he at length. "But I tell you truthfully, it proved effective."

"One more thing, Wallace."

"By all means."

"If it were possible, say, to replicate this potion you talk of, to produce a modern serum from the remains of this long-extinct tree-rat, who should possess the requisite skills, the knowledge, to carry it through?"

"The Chinese come to mind. As a race, they are so far advanced in alternative medicine. One only has to visit a Chinese herbalist in Limehouse to see the similarities."

The theatre lights dimmed. We took our places in the box. Alfred Wallace, his wife and family filed in and took their seats. Opera glasses close at hand, at last the performance was under way. A rousing overture, both instantly melodic and catchy, set our feet tapping and hands clapping to the infectious rhythm of the orchestra being conducted by Sir Penfold Wilkes in white tie and tails. A stirring baton-led march led to the curtains parting on an idyllic tropical island. A gorgeous young lady walked hand-in-hand beneath the coconut palms with her handsome beau and a love duet ensued.

"By Jove," said I to Alfred Wallace in the next seat, "that's the second catchy tune and we're barely into the first act."

"Agreed," said he, nodding his head, his spectacles flashing in the subdued lighting. "I think they have a success on their hands, Dr Watson."

Entranced, we sat in the box, occasionally moved to tears, as stirring rumbustious marches alternated with tuneful ballads and Bella eventually promised eternal fidelity and marriage to young Archie, a poor rating whose ship would be leaving for England the next day, leaving the pretty young maiden alone to pine for her love. She, the daughter of a cantankerous, possessive widower, a hypochondriac moaner, a gruff old Welsh missionary by the name of Davies, played to perfection by our dear friend Charles Lemon.

The first act went riotously well and we sat enthralled. The second act, however, seemed to fall short. I should mention, we were by then introduced to a chorus of cuddly dancing giant rats who sang of the delights of an idyllic tropical island. 'Sumatra, Sumatra, Sumatran jolly rats are we. Paradise is ours, the sun, the palms and the sea'.

Tosh, of course, but the younger members of the audience lapped it up, screaming and wildly applauding every time the blasted rodents made an appearance. I perceived the more mature members of the audience found the cuddly toy rats annoying after a while and I heard much coughing and blowing of noses.

The light opera, a musical entertainment in the style of Gilbert and Sullivan, else Franz Lehar, was well directed and had much to commend it. This said, those wretched singing and dancing giant rats spoiled it for me. I should rather have seen more of the beautiful, leggy chorus girls dressed in grass skirts.

By the last act, however, the musical had gloriously improved and even though the giant rats appeared in the finale, the final, uplifting duet where young Archie, now a naval lieutenant, returns to Sumatra and rescues Bella from the cooking pot, was superb. He sang poignantly the words: 'Sumatra, Sumatra, I met the love of my life here, I have eyes only for you dearest dear, dearest Bella, my sweetest Bella dear.'

This brought the house down. We all stood up and applauded. Everyone in the theatre was on their feet for a last rousing, foot-stomping rendition of the catchy overture.

After the last bow, the applause gently dying away while the house gas jets came up, we made our way downstairs to congratulate the composer, Christopher Chymes and lyricist Philip Troy, and break a bottle of champagne with the impresario of the Wimborne, Langton Lovell and his business partner Charles Lemon, who had played the old missionary, Davies, with such zeal. Unfortunately, a terrible tragedy then occurred, which marred proceedings somewhat.

Holmes and myself were being led along a backstage corridor full of props and actors congratulating one another, when – from a room at the end – a very shocked and pale-looking Christopher Chymes emerged, supported by Langton Lovell.

"Philip is dead," the composer gasped, tears forming in the corners of his eyes. "Poor Troy's dead."

"A heart failure," said I, rushing forward. "Christopher, I am a doctor, we may be able to yet resuscitate him."

"No point. He's been murdered," he cried. "Oh dear God, his throat's clawed through, there's so much blood – up the walls ... the lino. The room's been ransacked!"

"Steady, Christopher," said Langton, leading Chymes over to a props trunk, insisting he should sit down and gather composure. "Hurry!"

I was annoyed when a tall Chinamen in flowing robes, wearing a pill-box hat, barged right past us without a by-your-leave, dashing into the recently vacated murder room.

"Where is he? Where is my patient?" he said, more to himself than us, his noble Oriental features clouding over into a protracted scowl. His thin, cruel mouth pursed slightly. He shook his head and was about to depart through the crowd of horrified onlookers gathering in the corridor when, brandishing his sword stick, Holmes promptly blocked his path.

"Dr Wu Xing, I presume?" said my companion, peering into the Chinaman's face. "You will do me the honour of accompanying myself and Dr Watson back to Baker Street. We have much to discuss. If you want to avoid the police and remain at liberty I strongly advise you to comply. A four- wheeler shall convey us swiftly to Marylebone. Theatre land must, for now, be forsaken, perhaps prudent, for the Wimborne shall soon become awash with the denizens of Fleet Street and Scotland Yard to examine the murder scene. Do I make myself plain?"

"Undoubtedly. Come, gentlemen, I am no Malay or Chinese coolie from East India Docks, neither do I frequent the opium dens of Lime house. We are civilised human beings. Lead the way, Mr Sherlock Holmes. I have long been acquainted with your reputation as the capital's greatest serving consulting detective. Dr Watson, I feel privileged to meet you, albeit in questionable circumstances."

"Compliments and flattery aside, you are in very deep, Dr Wu. Your patient is, I believe, reliably responsible for two brutal murders in Norfolk and now this debacle, this bloodbath backstage at the Wimborne."

We flagged down a cab outside the theatre. There was mayhem, crowds of morbid sightseers descending on the Wimborne as though for a show of carnage at the Roman Coliseum. Word had got out that Philip Troy, responsible for writing the lyrics to the latest smash musical The Giant Rats of Sumatra, had been murdered back stage. I was glad to be quitting the West End, for it seemed to me, under the gas lamps, that people looked as ghoulish and hungry as marauding vampires, eager to be part of this event, to be involved and able to say, 'Look at me – I was there.' No, I confess I was glad to get out. No doubt Inspector Lustrade would be leading an investigation into the matter. Good luck to him. Holmes and myself had bigger fish to fry, for Dr Wu Xing represented a breakthrough. How I longed to hear what he had to relate concerning his controversial patient.

"A monster," the Chinaman murmured, smoking an exotic, perfumed cigarette from an ivory holder carved with writhing black bears locked in combat. Our four-wheeler rattled along Drury Lane towards High Holborn.

"Pardon me?" said I, peering out as the dun-coloured fog, less persistent, lifted in places so that I could see we were approaching Long Acre upon our left.

"A monster smash, Dr Watson. Nothing shall stop the publicity now. Demand for tickets shall be phenomenal."

"Indeed," remarked Holmes, puffing on his pipe as our cab clattered through foggy London, onwards towards Oxford Street.

Once in the familiar surroundings of our diggings, blinds drawn, lamps lit, a good fire raging in the grate, Holmes poured us a glass of whisky. He charged his long cherry-wood pipe with the strongest shag from the Persian slipper and, once he was sat cross-legged in his favourite armchair, began to probe the clever, if conceited, mind of the Chinese doctor of alternative medicine.

"You have a clinic, I believe?"

"Yes, in Mayfair – in a brick and stucco terrace off Regent Street."

"Plagiarism – stolen ideas – that's where part of the problem of this confounded multi-faceted puzzle of murder and bodily rejuvenation lies, is it not, Dr Wu Xing?"

"You are, of course, correct, Mr Holmes. The original idea for the light opera that I am sure both of you enjoyed this evening at the Wimborne, came from Ethby Sands. Perhaps you noticed a japanned upright piano he keeps in the bay of his sitting room at Albany. It possesses pleasant memories and has a very impressive history. When he first visited my clinic, he told me how, as a young man, he was a passable pianist. He could play Chopin, or a ragtime tune, for friends at a supper party. He was not of a professional standard – entirely self-taught.

"One winter's afternoon he claimed he saw the face of his long-dead mother in the gilt mirror and was instantly moved to sit on the stool and randomly play at scales. He swears, gentlemen, that in under ten minutes he composed a catchy hymn tune, that at first he was convinced he must have heard before at a concert or choral gathering. He wrote down the music upon the back of a cigarette packet and thought no more of it until, when entertaing some fellow residents in Albany, he played it to the conductor Lonsdale Chymes, who instantly said he had a smash. The rest, as they say, is music publishing history. The Americans loved it, church choirs loved it, orchestras performed the piece, and even today it remains a popular tune played in front rooms throughout the land. Boosey & Hawkes have so far sold thirty million copies of the sheet music – and counting. The title 'Take Thy Tiny Hand in Mine' was likewise Ethby's, who of course wrote both words and music to his 'little ditty', as he fondly referred to the hymn."

"So Christopher's father, Lonsdale, forms a link. It was the famous orchestra conductor who advised Ethby Sands, and you could say was partly responsible for the tune's success?" asked Holmes.

"Lonsdale, through his music contacts, championed the song. He was very generous in his praise of the hymn and must have helped its path considerably," replied Dr Wu.

"But the son, Christopher, who himself resides at Albany ...?"

"Listen," sighed Wu, "that plain and simple hymn dwarfed any of the achievements of Christopher Chymes and Philip Troy. A modest reputation they had as a songwriting team, certainly. They'd played as a duo at the Ritz and small venues, showcasing their material. But neither had hit the big money and wanted in on celebrity and fame. However, neither Chymes nor Troy had a core idea, something to get theatre producers and impresarios knocking at their door. One evening, they had a bachelor's supper with Ethby Sands at his upstairs set. He was, of course, at the time an M.P. for Norwich and busy with affairs of constituency and Parliament. There was even talk that one day he might become a cabinet minister.

"Anyhow, thinking them fake, he got up and played them a tune and – foolishly he admits this, somewhat tight from too much wine and champagne, confided to them his gay and romping tour de force, a light opera set on a paradise island in Indonesia – the island of Sumatra."

"And this is where Alfred Russell Wallace comes in," said I, understanding at last.

"Charles Darwin was offered an animal hide, purportedly belonging to a now extinct species of Sumatran tree-rat – an enormous rodent. Thinking them faked, he decided to sell. Once the property of the naturalist and explorer Alfred Wallace, who recently returned to England after a lengthy sojourn in the tropics, a London dealer was the first choice, but in the end Ethby Sands purchased these extraordinary items for one hundred guineas. He kept them displayed in a glass cabinet – a curiosity – a conversation piece. People would glance at the mummified rat – comment on it. But when Ethby Sands came to be gravely ill, near death, and all the specialists in Harley Street had given up on him, he remembered its curious and spectacular provenance."

"I must be frank, Dr Wu, I already interview Alfred Wallace. At the Royal Geographical Society I have seen the rat, drawn on a sixteenth-century Portuguese map – a caricature of a giant rat, dis- turbingly and horribly portrayed by the illustra- tor. I can only draw the following conclusion. Somehow, you and your team of microscopic chemists, who are specialised practitioners of Chinese alternative medicine, have managed to duplicate the Indonesian shaman's anti-ageing formula, based on grinding the bone of this long extinct creature to form a compound of fine pow- der to which you add further ingredients.

"At a time when Mr Sands virtually gave up hope, as a last resort he visited your radical clinic in Mayfair, and you and your team able to keep his wasting illness at bay, make him a young man again. But what you had not taken into account was the addictive nature of the serum and the fact it produced terrible side-effects, the rats genes gradually infecting, eventually taking over his physical self, for periods making him volatile, unbelievably aggressive. Wu Xing, you have created a person who, when dominated by this Sumatran rat's genes, will kill mercilessly. "When I first examined my patient, he was fifty- three, but aged beyond his years, the ravages of the illness having left him in a wheelchair, almost without energy to eat properly. 'Go to my rented house in Norfolk – Foxbury Hall – money is no object. You have the old rat's skin and bone, the provenance, the handwritten account by my dear friend Alfred Wallace detailing his miraculous recovery, the life-giving force for renewal. Do it before it is too late. You have my complete trust. I am confident you will succeed."

Not long after this episode, we received an invitation, as did Dr Wu and Christopher Chymes, to attend cocktails at No.32 Albany. We were grim and pensive when, on a cold and dank November day, we were shown upstairs to Sands' exclusive set. Welcoming us, Sands, wearing polished red

loafers, tartan stockings, an exclusive green tweed suit and a gold fob watch-chain in his waistcoat, was charm itself, politely taking our hats, coats and walking sticks, and ushering us into the sitting room with its glass display cases full of stuffed red birds of paradise.

There, above the mantelpiece, was the same gilt-framed portrait in oils I had seen the last time I was here. Ethby Sands, M.P., painted at the House of Commons. By his careworn expression, heavy jowls, pouches beneath the eyes, grey hair and grizzled side-whiskers, and the wrinkled folds of skin about his scrawny neck, I should have placed his age in the portrait at pushing on eight-and- fifty, and yet here he was unsettlingly in the flesh, stood over by the Chinese Chippendale chair, looking at most twenty-one years old. I confess, it was hard to fathom we were in the presence of a monster who had already cold-bloodedly killed three people, two of them in Norfolk, and who, by usage of a controversial serum, was enabled to stay young and active, staving off the effects of ageing and ultimately his own death from a wasting disease.

"This just can't continue," said Dr Wu, ever noble and calm in a crisis, this in the face of a dangerously volatile patient who could at any time change into a violent, rabid animal. "Come to my Mayfair clinic. I can offer you renewed detoxification. We can at least stabilise your condition and prevent further unfortunate mishaps occurring."

His eyes twinkled with perception. "My physician speaks eloquently and wisely," remarked Ethby Sands, lighting an Egyptian cigarette. "Gentlemen, help yourselves to whisky, we shall toast my imminent demise. I shall myself abstain from alcohol."

"I mean our imminent demise, Mr Holmes, for you and your compatriots are about to join me in a final, wondrous climax to my life. Regard, if you will, the japanned upright piano over in the bay, on which I composed a popular hymn, still in vogue after all these years. Thirty million copies of sheet music sold and still counting. My valet, Garson, visiting one of his lady friends in the vicinity of Soho, I have conceived of a means of destruction, both spellbinding and futuristic, which I am sure you will applaud for its ingenuity.

"I myself have created a lethal piano, and here's how it works. You will, each of you, in turn step forward and play a white or black note of your choosing on the keyboard. We, gentlemen, are about to embark upon a game of 'musical Russian roulette', because one of the notes on my little piano, when struck, will accordingly blow us all to kingdom come and destroy Albany forever, together with my other esteemed residents who share this most prestigious of London addresses. My piano keys are linked to several bundles of dynamite. I shall not give too much away, lest our sleuth-hound, Mr Holmes, using that damn clever brain of his, outwits its workings. I think you'll agree I've not been idle. If you fail to come forward and take your turn, I shall shoot you point blank, with this pair of sophisticated silver repeater pistols I purchased from Naysmith of St James earlier. Are we all clear?"

"Perfectly so," remarked Holmes. "May I smoke?"

"Of course. I shall allow a ten minute interval before we begin – enough time, I'm sure, to concentrate your minds and prepare for your imminent demise, just as I had to do when I was languishing in my wheeled chair when those Harley Street doctors gave me but a fortnight to live. Alas, I must report the serum Dr Wu developed in Norfolk will become depleted and I shall feel all the effects of accelerating old age and bodily collapse, which I am loath to endure, the wasting disease returning with a vengeance. No shaman, or potion, will be able to protect me from that. Why, Chymes, you will be first to play a note on my piano. I see you're trembling already. This only increases my enjoyment of the proceedings. You plagiarised my ideas, after all."

"One moment, if I may, Sands. Might I clear up a few points?" Holmes asked, puffing on his pipe. "Of course, Mr Holmes. I should be glad to answer any questions. But only eight-and-a-half minutes remain, so be brief.

"The miraculous transformation brought about by the serum developed by Dr Wu and his team of microscopic chemists in the privacy of Norfolk, the undisputed fact that, after a course of injections, you – a middle-aged man – became young again after spending virtually a year as a crotchety old invalid. So you were, one morning, able to simply get up from your wheeled chair, put on your red loafers, and walk out of the door."

"Dear me, we only have a couple of minutes remaining. A glass of lemon bitters, if you please, Dr Wu. I am all of a sudden grown weary of this conversation."

"Allow me," said Holmes, stepping behind me and pouring from a carafe.

"Drink it all down, Sands," said the Oriental physician kindly, giving his patient a confident stare. "Your blood sugars must be low. The lemon bitters will refresh you, the quinine perk you up a bit."

"Yes, a tonic is all I require," he agreed, taking the glass from Holmes and draining it before placing it upon the sideboard. "Dr Wu Xing," said he, with a sudden rush of passion, "I owe you so much. Despite everything that has happened, I always value our friendship. Please allow me to extend my ..."

All of us, the Chinaman included, looked on astonished as Ethby Sands, seized by an apoplectic fit, pitched forward, his eyes bulging, before landing at our feet, quite dead. Sprawled on the rug, he lay perfectly still, very much the corpse, aptly surrounded by glass-fronted cabinets containing his stuffed collection. His beloved japanned upright piano remained untested, the lid firmly closed upon the keys by Christopher Chymes. The exclusive Albany would not be obliterated in a frightful explosion, nor us, thank heavens, its tenants.

"Cyanide is a remarkably swift-acting poison," my illustrious colleague remarked, striking a match to his ever-present pipe. "While Dr Watson obscured me, I was able to empty a sachet into the carafe. One always prefers to come to these types of meetings prepared. We had better inform the porter downstairs, to put out an urgent request for an undertaker. We shall, of course, require a death certificate, which Watson thoughtfully brought along in his wallet. Dr Wu, you will please act as witness to the signature."

"I should be honoured," he exclaimed, addressing my friend with a majestic bow, for the first time his thin, cruel lips breaking into the faintest smile. "Although, as a man of science, a practising physician, I should much prefer ..."

"To retain his body for further analysis and research into your nefarious anti-ageing serum? I'm afraid, Dr Wu, that would be out of the question. Might I further enquire about a compostable lightweight coffin, a wickerwork shell observed in the billiard room at Foxbury Hall at the end of October?"

"I use these for conveying difficult patients who, by means of acupuncture, I induce into a state of deep rest and place in the shell. We can move a patient from A to B very effectively. Once more, my Mayfair clinic's superior advances in patient care come to the fore, Mr Holmes."

"So this is presumably how Mr Sands was removed from Foxbury Hall and travelled down to London?"

"Indeed."

The autumnal gales, the spell of wet and windy weather in London was succeeded by a static, impenetrable pea-souper. The dun-coloured fog blanketed the capital, refusing to budge for days making travelling unpredictable. At least our chimney had ceased to smoke and we were no longer susceptible to sudden gusts of wind dislodging soot into our grate.

"The new musical at the Wimborne has been feted by the critics as 'an unstoppable success'," said I, turning over the pages of my Daily Telegraph while Mrs Hudson cleared away the breakfast things. My companion merely assented.

"Lovell and Lemon must be congratulated," he answered. "Broadway beckons. To have achieved a move to New York in such a short space of time is extraordinary. I suppose Christopher Chymes must be lapping up the adulation."

“And raking in the big money,” I answered.

The Sherlock Holmes Series

Sherlock by the Sea

Sherlock Holmes & the Wheelchair Mob

www.ingramcontent.com/pod-product-compliance
Lightning Source LLC
Chambersburg PA
CBHW051139190726
48290CB00006B/1911